the windfarmer

by Chris Wichtendahl

CONTENTS

CHAPTER 1

I t was late at night, the time of night that's technically morning, and in a sparsely comfortable Metro apartment, Jase Logan was sleeping.

He really shouldn't have been sleeping. He should have, at that exact moment, been in the process of getting shocked awake by an unpleasantly loud alarm going off directly inside his skull. The alarm should have been going off, because, at that exact moment, hundreds of miles west of Jase Logan's sparsely comfortable Metro apartment, something alarming was happening.

More accurately, the alarming thing had already happened, and the alarms that alert people when alarming things happen were now alerting certain people. One such alarm was the one that should have been going off inside Jase Logan's skull. If it had, he would have gotten up, remotely logged into his work terminal, and let the alarm know he'd been alerted, so no one else, certainly not his boss, needed to be woken up in a similar fashion.

Unfortunately for Jase, he'd long since deactivated his alarm, based on the fact that most of the time people just ticked the necessary boxes to make the alarms shut up and then dealt with whatever the alarm was about in the morning, and he figured he could skip that whole waking up and ticking boxes part and be more rested when he finally dealt with things in the morning. Therefore, he continued sleeping peacefully while, across town, his boss was woken up by an unpleasantly loud alarm going off in her skull. The first thing she did, after dragging herself out of bed, logging into her terminal and telling the alarm to please shut up, was ping Jase to find out where the hell he was and why the alarm had escalated to her. However, Jase had also disabled all incoming call functions, so his pleasant slumber continued unabated.

Later, Jase Logan woke when and how he usually did, blissfully unaware of the events of the previous night.

"Jase," a pleasant soft voice said, "wake up."

Jase Logan grunted and rolled over.

"Jase," the voice sounded exactly the same, only slightly louder, "wake up."

Jase moaned, burrowing into his pillow.

"Jase," the voice was more insistent, and even louder, "wake up!"

"Snooze."

"You have disabled the snooze function on this apartment's alarm protocol," the voice informed him, still just as loud.

"Override," Jase mumbled.

"Unauthorized," the voice said. "Ten seconds until alarm protocol enters cacophonous phase." The voice began counting down.

At three, Jase sat up and swung his legs over the side of the bed. "Alright!" he shouted. "I'm up! See?" he pointed to his feet. "I'm awake!"

"Good morning, Jase," the voice had returned to its original soft and pleasant tone.

Jase yawned and stretched, ignoring the popping and cracking sounds his body made.

"Morning, apartment," he said. He sat on the edge of the bed a moment.

"You have several urgent work messages awaiting your attention," the apartment informed him.

He yawned again, then stood. "Yeah," he said, "I guess I should go into the office, then. Start shower," he said, with another yawn. "Then begin stim and nutrient shake prep. I'll deal with whatever it is when I get there." He shuffled sleepily to the bathroom to begin his morning routine.

As he showered, the apartment began an ambient news feed.

The hearings in Washington over the Confederacy's alleged sheltering of Christian militants continued. The Confederate senator debated the validity of the accusations, demanding proof that her government was turning a blind eye to militant camps in the mountains near their border with the Appalachian territory. She also demanded, as a condition of any action, that the Midland Republic work harder to shut down the actions of the Parish Coven, whom she claimed operated with impunity within their borders.

"Right," Jase muttered, lathering up. "Best of luck with all *that*. Washington has as much power as I do to force the American nations to do anything. Change."

The news changed to a local report of the ongoing cleanup efforts in the Metro Boglands. Jase wondered why they bothered. He, like most Metro residents living in Manhattan, thought the toxic swamps encompassing what used to be eastern New Jersey were the only things keeping their backward neighbors in the Jersey hill country at bay. "Change," he said, rinsing off.

The CEO of Lance Entertainment had no comment on a vid-stream star's supposed overdose at the Pleasure Dome resort island in the center of the Florida Sea. A spokesperson for the media giant said the actress in question had succumbed to heatstroke as she and her family enjoyed the attractions of the resort's sprawling theme park. She was currently being treated on-site by their medical staff and was expected to make a full recovery.

"Change." Jase turned off the water and toweled himself dry.

IRISCorp (Integrated Responsive Information Systems Corporation) was revealing their latest technological marvel. However, like most of their recent product launches, it was really just a minor upgrade to their last one. Since the first EndoTech device debuted a decade earlier, people had gone from a healthy skepticism toward a device that involved implanting circuitry inside their bodies, to rabidly awaiting each upgrade. The Endo 7 series would boast shorter charging times, increased kinetic power supply, a streamlined display, and faster data transfer speeds (network permitting). Jase hung his towel on the bathroom door and walked back to his bedroom.

"Change." He dressed and ran his fingers through his damp hair. With a quick glance in the mirror, he declared it good enough. At almost forty years old, Jase was happy he still had most of his hair. He figured if he just let it do what it wanted, it wouldn't feel inclined to leave. He smoothed the front of his shirt and nodded approvingly at his reflection. His boss might not be happy about all the remote work he'd been doing, but it gave him plenty of time to work out. He flexed a bicep, then felt stupid and stopped. "Apartment," he said, pausing the news feed.

"Jase?"

"Infuse the stim into my shake and prepare it to go, then summon transport."

"Yes, Jase."

While he waited, Jase grabbed his Endo from its charging plate and inserted it into the docking port embedded in his left arm. He felt the usual tingle up his arm to his head, then a display was delivered directly to his optic nerve, making it appear to be floating in the air in front of him. His fingertips vibrated, indicating that his haptic sensors were active. An alert flashed in the corner of his display, insisting that there really was something quite urgent he should be dealing with. He shrugged and dismissed the alert. Probably some meeting or other. He committed himself anew to dealing with it later.

"Transport is outside," the apartment informed him. "Stim-shake is ready."

"Good." Jase grabbed the sealed cup from its nook in the kitchen, pressed a button on its side, and took a sip. Caffeinated nutrient shake didn't taste great, but he'd had worse. He pressed the button again to reseal the cup, tossed it in his bag, and headed out. The apartment locked itself behind him when he left.

He stepped out of the elevator into the lobby of his building. Sunlight streamed in through small windows set high up in the walls, as well as through the double glass doors at the top of a small flight of stairs. Water trickled down the stairs through the doors. He crossed the lobby, climbed carefully up the wet stairs, and walked through the double doors onto the floating walkway outside his building. A small boat was docked at the edge, waiting for him. He stepped into the boat and sat down as the driver undocked from the walkway.

"40th and 6th?" she asked. It was the address his apartment had sent.

"That's right."

She swung the boat out into the 30th Street canal. They were going with the cross-town current, so they made good time, but it was time they'd lose batting the downtown current when they made 6th Avenue. As she turned into the uptown side of the canal, the driver swore at a young man on a small water-scooter, who was weaving between the larger boats, jumping his smaller craft over the chop of the rough current.

"Stupid fucking kids," the driver muttered. She glanced back at Jase. "Sorry, sir."

"Not at all," Jase waved it away. "Fuck him."

She smiled and continued uptown.

Jase looked out the window at the floating pavilions anchored between the uptown and downtown sides of the canal. Vessels of all sizes were docked at the pavilions, which sold anything from food to knick-knacks, to cheap knock-offs of just about any luxury item imaginable. Jase gulped down his shake while the driver navigated the busy morning rush.

Finally, the boat pulled up alongside National Consolidated's headquarters. Jase's transit app pinged, and the tip window opened in his display. He tapped a generous tip and closed the window, hopping out and onto the floating walkway.

"Thanks," the driver smiled at him.

Jase sketched a rough salute. "Have a good one," he said.

"You too," she replied, speeding off into the canal.

He looked up. On a clear day like today, it was sometimes possible to see the signal-drone swarms. The signal-drones had been built decades prior and flew several miles up. They were the reason people could get a high-power connection to the myriad private and public data networks available to their Endos and other connected devices. Jase watched a swarm in its migratory pattern of complex geometric shapes for a few moments before entering the lobby of National's headquarters.

Much like the lobby of his building, and all buildings in the old Boroughs of New York Metro, the windows were set high in the wall, to allow for raising the doors and eventually the floor as the water rose outside. He passed through the security gate, which pinged his Endo, and made his way to the elevator. It also pinged his Endo, automatically rising to his floor.

He stepped out of the elevator into a scene of quiet activity. Everyone was in their glass-walled offices, their Endos synced to their terminals, working diligently. Jase approached his, and noticed his office-mate, Alen, was already in.

"Hey," the younger man said, "if it isn't the mysterious Jase Logan. I thought you were going to work remotely until they forgot you worked here and stopped paying you."

Jase laughed, sitting down and syncing his Endo. "Yeah," he said. "That's kinda why I'm in the office today. Figured that was a real possibility."

"Stim?" Alen asked.

"Had some with my shake," Jase said, "but I'll walk over with you."

The two men walked to the small kitchen area off the main floor of office cubes, where a stim-prep and nutrient dispenser were located. A refrigerator was there for people who brought lunches and for any leftover catered food.

"You see *Electrospeedster* last night?" Alen asked.

"Yeah," Jase said. "That was really cool. I was hoping they'd do Tomorrow City this season."

"Right?" Alen punched the buttons for sweet and creamy. "It's not as cool as the old cartoon, though."

"Well," Jase said, grabbing a bottle of water from the dispenser, "they were never going to be able to do *that*. I thought they did as well as they could have."

"True," Alen said. He took a sip of his stim. "Oh!" he said. "Guess what Jenn and I had over the weekend."

"No."

Alen laughed. "Asshole. Anyway," he said, "we had real coffee."

"What?" Jase shook his head. "No way. What is there, like, one functioning coffee plantation left?" He took a sip if his water as they walked back toward their office.

"Okay," Alen said, "it wasn't real *fresh* coffee. Jenn's sister got her hands on a brick of the old freeze-dried stuff."

"Where?"

"You know those survival bunker auctions?"

"Yeah," Jase said.

"Apparently that's something she does, goes to these things and bids on all this weird old stuff. Anyway, this one had bricks of freeze-dried coffee. So," he said, "she brought some over and made it for us."

"And?"

Alen shrugged. "Eh," he said. "I don't know what the big deal was. Tasted like jet fuel poured from a horse's asshole."

"And you know what that tastes like?"

Alen laughed. "Long story."

"Please don't ever tell it to me."

"Oh shit!" Alen said as they arrived at their office. "Did you hear about what happened?"

"No," Jase said. "I saw some messages in my work queue, but figured I'd read them when I got to my desk. What's up?"

"We had a desertion," Alen said.

"A desertion?" An uneasy feeling crept its way up Jase's spine. "Where?"

"One of our energy farms out west," Alen said. "An indentured windfarmer."

Jase looked over at him, as the uneasy feeling got bored with climbing Jase's spine and dropped hard into his stomach instead, where it had itself a good swim and grew into a healthy sense of dread. "Uh," Jase cleared his throat. "Do, um, do you happen to know which farm, by any chance?"

"LOGAN!" a woman's voice roared across the office.

"Ah," Jase said, the sense of dread really getting comfortable in his stomach now. "Never mind."

Dela Chancellor, Director of Asset Management in Human Resources, strode purposefully and menacingly toward Jase. She was half his size, ten years his junior, and her purposeful stride normally sent people scurrying out of her way. Her menacing one sent them hiding in their offices. Both at once had most people wondering if it were still possible to buy a decent survival bunker, and how far away they could manage to build it. "My office," she growled at Jase as she passed, ignoring Alen completely.

Jase sat in a chair in Dela's office, while she sat across her desk from him, visibly trying to compose herself.

Jase wondered whether talking or remaining silent would make that easier.

"Jase," she said finally, with a tone that made it very clear she'd been up since an hour so far removed from when she usually woke up, it was only her extreme exhaustion that had saved Jase from being thrown off the roof of the building.

"I--"

She held up her hand, and the look on her face suggested that, even though she was so tired she could barely think straight, let alone drag a man twice her size up to the roof and throw him off, she'd be willing to give it a go. "Jase," she said again, this time with a weary sigh thrown in, "where the hell were you last night?"

Jase swallowed. "I, um..."

She sighed again, pinching the bridge of her nose and slowly shaking her head. "Oh, please don't tell me you were asleep."

"Fine," Jase said, trying on a smile. "I won't tell you."

Dela raised both eyebrows so high, they could have introduced themselves to her hairline. "Jokes?" was all she said.

Jase put away the smile, opting for something more contrite. "Sorry," he said.

"You should be," Dela told him. "You turned off your alarm?!"

"I figured it was--"

She held up her hand again. "I don't care," she said. She went silent and just stared at him, with an expression Jase couldn't entirely figure out, beyond the fact that it was not meant to be friendly. "I think I've been incredibly patient with you, Jase," she said at last.

Jase nodded. That seemed the best course at this point.

"All the remote work, the lack of initiative..."

"I do good work," Jase protested.

"You do *adequate* work," Dela said, glaring at him, and it occurred to Jase he'd been better off with the nodding. "You've spent five years as a mid-level Asset Manager doing adequate work. How long did you think you were going to get away with that?"

"Well..." Jase had actually thought he'd be able to get away with it indefinitely.

"Stop talking," Dela said.

Jase shut his mouth.

Dela looked at him again. Her expression softened, but it was into a look of pity that Jase had seen far too many times. Anger was almost preferable, but as anger would likely lead to firing at best, and something more permanent at worst, he decided pity was probably his best option. "Look, Jase," she said, her voice also softening ever so slightly. "I've let you coast the past few years because... well..." she shrugged.

He nodded again. "Yeah..."

"But this..." she shook her head. "I can't ignore this, Jase."

"I know."

"This is a desertion," she said. "Do you know how long it's been since the last one of those we've had?"

Jase opened his mouth to answer.

"Long enough for people above my pay grade, and *way* above yours, to start getting very angry."

He nodded.

"So," she said, with another weary sigh, "I've booked you an open ticket out of the South Bay transit hub. It expires at midnight, so you'd better be well on your way by then."

Jase saw an alert at the corner of his Endo display. He assumed it was the ticket. He blinked at her. "I don't understand."

"I covered for you with the execs," she said. "I did the job you were supposed to do, and told them I'd given you permission to turn your alarms off for the night."

"Why?"

"Because I want to give you one last chance," she said. She looked him in the eyes, and he felt guilty over the dark circles around hers. "Get your ass out to that windfarm, find that indenture, and get him back to work. Alen will coordinate from here."

Jase looked down at his lap, then back up at her. "Dela, I..."

"Save it," she said. "This is your last chance. Get this done, quickly and quietly, or don't bother coming back." She sat back and focused on her Endo display, indicating she was done talking to him.

He nodded and got up from his seat, leaving her office without another word.

CHAPTER 2

The official name on maps was The Commonwealth of New England. The southern nations referred to it as The Yankee Commonwealth, though it was usually just 'the Commonwealth' in everyday conversation. It was the only nation that still regularly taxed its citizens, with a higher tax rate for corporate entities, per an amendment in its constitution, following the First Corporate War. For that reason, and its tendency toward government regulation, the Commonwealth had few, if any, corporate headquarters within its borders. What it did have, however, was the most efficient and extensive system of mass transit on the American continent, which it operated in partnership with the neighboring Midland Republic. If anyone wished to travel from the east coast to any point west with any dependability, they would first travel north to one of several transport hubs in the Commonwealth. There they could take any manner of public transport as far as the western border of the Republic. At that point, most travelers were at the mercy of the various corporate transit services that ran through the plains and deserts of the West. Fortunately for Jase, he worked for the parent company of several such transit services, so he would have little trouble reaching the windfarm from his final train stop.

He stepped off the ferry he'd taken from the Manhattan canals onto a dock at the southernmost transit hub in the Commonwealth. His Endo display flashed at the corner of his eye. It was informing him that he was leaving the jurisdiction of his corporate citizenship and entering a non-affiliated nation, where he would have little to no immunity under local or national laws. This didn't bother him very much. For one thing, he was well beyond his lawless youth. For another, he wouldn't be in the Commonwealth long enough to run afoul of their laws, had he been so inclined.

He flicked the alert away and looked around. This transit hub, being at such a low elevation, was composed of several floating docks of various sizes, along with anchored pavilions. The train tracks were all on bridges that kept them high enough above the water to allow for its continued rise. He made his way from his dock, across a few others, until he was standing on one of the pavilions. He tapped on his Endo display and opened a map of the station. A blue line superimposed itself over his surroundings, and he followed it up several flights of stairs, across three more pavilions, and through the crowded labyrinthine terminals of the station. He always felt claustrophobic in crowds, though the open nature of the hub was ameliorating the sensation somewhat. He passed by a young woman playing the accordion along with a prerecorded track, a few jugglers, and four people performing a one-act play. They were all quite good. One didn't busk the Commonwealth hubs without the talent to back it up. He passed by a fire-eater and two acrobats, the map leading him steadily north until he reached the appropriate train terminal. It was a simple matter to find his track, and he even had time to buy a nutrient bar and a bottle of water while he waited for his train to be ready.

While he waited, he looked over the file Dela had sent him about the fugitive windfarmer. His name was Jan Hollis. He looked to be only a few years younger than Jase, and according to his file, was an excellent worker. Apparently, the day before he'd left, a young woman had arrived at the farm; a refugee from Appalachia named Moira Townes. The file included a picture of her as well. She had the prematurely aged look most of the refugees had, and the look of weary, malnourished fear that tended to be on everyone's faces outside the wealthier nations. There'd been an incident with a few of the other workers, Hollis had gotten involved, then the next morning, they were both gone. Jase shook his head. Hollis was nearly done with his indenture. Deserting now made no sense. What could have made him do it?

Eventually they called for boarding and he approached the train. A conductor pinged his Endo, scanned his single bag, and gestured for him to proceed to the economy car. Usually, National employees traveled in business class private compartments, but apparently Dela wanted to make a point, and he was riding the two-day trip in a coach seat. He sighed, gripped his bag, and made his way onto the train.

A few hours later, he sat at a table in the dining car, impressed as he often was with the quality of the food. He had just finished his salad and was waiting for his main course when an older woman sat down across from him.

"Hello," she said. "I hope you don't mind, but they told me I had to sit here."

Jase nodded and smiled. "They need to conserve space," he said, "so they put people together who wouldn't fill a table on their own." He offered his hand. "I'm Jase. Jase Logan." He was being far more gregarious than he usually felt when paired with a stranger, but experience had taught him that his usual demeanor of shy awkwardness sprinkled with esoteric sarcasm made for unpleasantness all around, and everyone's meal went down much easier if he affected an attitude of friendly politeness instead.

"Nice to meet you, Jase," she shook his hand. "Miranda Shah."

"A pleasure, Miranda."

"So," she said, "do they do that for every meal, or is that something special?"

"They've done it every meal I've ever had on the train," he said.

"Really?" she asked. "Oh, thank you," she said to the young woman who brought her salad. She asked Jase, "Do you ride the train often?"

Jase nodded. "I travel out west for business about once a year," he said.

"You must meet some very interesting people in this car."

He shrugged. "More or less," he said. "Most people end up being very pleasant to share a meal with. Others..." he shivered dramatically, "not as much."

"Oh dear," she said, covering a grin. "I hope I'm not one of those."

"So far, so good," he said with a smile. "How am I doing?"

"As polite and charming as a lady could hope, Mr. Logan," she said, returning the smile.

Their meals arrived, and they ate in silence for a few moments. Jase took a sip of water and said, "So, is this your first time on a train?"

She nodded. "For such a long journey, at least. I'm visiting my daughter in Cincinnati. I usually take the bus."

Jase's eyes widened. "A bus ride from the Commonwealth to the central Midlands?" He shook his head. "That can't be fun." The transit services of the Commonwealth, and to a slightly lesser degree the Midlands, were efficient and well-staffed, with top-of-the-line equipment and highly-skilled operators. That being said, no one in the history of human civilization had ever managed to make riding the bus a pleasant experience.

She grinned. "It isn't. But," she said, "this time I'm visiting for a very special occasion. My daughter just had a baby."

"Congratulations," Jase said, toasting her with his water bottle.

"Thank you," she said. "He's my first grandchild, and my daughter and her wife decided I should travel out to meet him in style, so they splurged on a sleeper compartment for me." She took a drink of water. "It's quite comfortable."

"More than you'd think, right?" Jase thought of all the other times he'd made this trip, and the comfortable private compartment he slept in. Then he thought about the seat waiting for him in coach, and the slovenly mouth-breather in the seat next to it, who had an unfortunate habit of leaning in very close when he talked, which was constantly, and the fact that said mouth-breather had only rudimentary understanding of the basic concept of hygiene.

"You said you travel out west on business," Miranda said, bringing his attention back to the table. "What business is that?"

"I'm an HR representative for National Consolidated," he said.

"Really?" she asked. "I wouldn't think someone from HR would have to travel so much."

"Normally, no," he said. "But every year I make a trip out west to inspect our energy farms, to make sure our indentured employees are being treated well, and the farms are acting in accordance with international law." He tried not to grimace at that. His diligence in that area was spotty, at best. He usually just passed through each farm, assumed everyone was doing their best, and made the most of the trip.

"Indentures?" a slight reserve came over her then, and she became very interested in the contents of her plate. "Oh."

"You don't approve." It wasn't a question.

"Oh no," she said, looking up. "It's not that, it's just... well," she considered, "I suppose I don't." Her face flushed as she looked at him. "I'm so sorry," she said. "I don't mean to offend you, I know it's your job..."

"Not at all," he said, offering a professional smile. He wasn't surprised. The Commonwealth had always been vehemently anti-indenture, considering it little more than, as one of their representatives put it, 'tidied-up corporate-speak for slavery'. "It's... a complicated issue," he said.

"Is it?"

Jase nodded. "It can be."

The young woman came and gathered their plates, asking if they wanted stim or dessert. Jase ordered stim. He was fairly certain Miranda would take this opportunity to leave the table.

She did. After assuring the young woman that she didn't want anything, she tapped at the air, leaving a tip through her Endo, then stood. "It was nice meeting you, Mr. Logan," she said. "For the record," she went on, looking him directly in the eyes, "it's not that complicated. You seem a pleasant enough young man, but, I must say --"

"I get it," Jase said.

"I don't think you do," she said. She smiled then, as though just realizing how lecturing her tone had become toward a total stranger. "But, as I said, you seem like a decent man, so I'm sure you will. Good night, Mr. Logan."

He checked a weary sigh. "Good night, Ms. Shah."

She left. A few minutes later, the waitress returned with his stim.

These sorts of encounters didn't usually bother him so much, but in light of the desertion, it had caused him to think hard about his job and how he did it. He knew that whatever had caused Hollis to desert was something he would have caught during an inspection if he had actually been doing his job properly. Dela's words came back to him, and he thought that 'adequate' may have been too generous.

CHAPTER 3

I t was late the next day when Jase finally arrived at the windfarm, rumpled and tired. The car that picked him up at the station drove past the farm toward the nearby town, and Jase stared at the acres of turbines, their gently turning blades limned in the oranges and reds of the setting sun. The sun was almost to the horizon when the car pulled up in front of Jase's hotel, and already the streets were filling up with workers in matching coveralls, heading home from their shifts.

The town was wholly owned and run by National Consolidated and was home to a bustling square filled with shops, restaurants, and bars, along with a theater, library, and museum. Every corporate town had a museum, and they were essentially nothing but giant advertisements and propaganda for the company. They were usually sparsely attended, aside from the mandatory field trips taken by elementary school children once a year. The car drove past the empty museum, through the square, past the rows of apartment buildings that served as worker dormitories, and stopped at an old hotel at the edge of the apartment blocks, just before the start of a small residential neighborhood. Most of the houses were home to farm management and those who ran businesses in town.

Jase stepped out of the car and looked up at the chipped and weathered facade. Bandwidth modules had been bolted on to the building over the decades, enabling even faster and stronger connection to the swarms of signal-drones overhead. Most public accommodation had such modules. Free, high-speed data connection was a valued amenity. Jase looked closely, near one cluster of modules, and could just make out the faint outlines left by the old logo of whatever hotel chain had last owned the building. He couldn't tell much about it, and it wouldn't have mattered if it had still hung on the side of the building. It probably belonged to a company that went under during the First Corporate War. He spared the faded remnant a last glance and walked through the large sliding doors into the lobby. The hotel was used primarily for visiting executives, people like Jase, and prospective employees. The doorway pinged his Endo as he walked through, and he was met by a young woman in hotel livery.

"Mr. Logan," she said, "welcome to Turbine Conglomerate Forty-Seven. We hope you enjoy your stay in Consolidated Temporary Housing. Will you require a key?" Her smile was warm and welcoming, but not so much that it would be mistaken for genuine.

"The doors have readers?" he assumed they did.

"Of course, sir."

"Then I'll be fine."

"Very good, sir," she said. "Do you need help with your bag?"

He hefted his single bag on his shoulder and smiled. "I'll manage."

"Excellent." Her smile widened exactly enough. "I hope your time here is productive. Ping the front desk if you need anything."

He nodded and she walked off. He took an elevator up to the fourth floor and followed the map that had appeared in his display. He placed his hand against a panel next to the door of his room. He felt his fingertips buzz, and the door clicked open.

The room was small, sparsely furnished, and tastefully decorated. A double bed was flanked by two end tables, a desk sat in one corner, and an armchair in another. A doorway led to a small efficiency bathroom, and the closet contained a small dresser. He tossed his bag onto the armchair and sat on the bed. He wasn't due to visit the farm until the next day, so he decided to take a quick shower and see some of the town before turning in.

Later, he approached the front desk, clean, freshly shaved, and dressed in casual business attire. The young woman who'd greeted him when he arrived was there. She was looking at something on her Endo, but brought her attention back around when he moved into her field of vision.

"Mr. Logan," she said with her standard smile, blinking slightly as her eyes adjusted to visual input rather than direct stimulation from her Endo. "Heading out for a night on the town, are we?"

"Well," he smiled back, "as much of a night on the town as one can have here on a Tuesday night with a meeting on Wednesday morning. Can you recommend a decent place to eat?"

"Of course, sir," she said. "There are three places that serve food in town. One of them just does breakfast and lunch, so they're closed. That leaves Family Bistro and the Corner Tavern." She thought a moment. "I mostly go to the Corner Tavern," she said. "It's a decent place with good food. It has a bar, and live music on weekends."

"I assume Family Bistro speaks for itself?" Jase grinned.

She nodded. "Families with kids as far as the eye can see, and no bar."

"Corner Tavern it is, then."

She glanced around briefly, then leaned forward, her voice dropping to a whisper. "Um, we're not really supposed to recommend this place, since it's not operated by the company..."

"But..." he raised an eyebrow.

"But if you're looking for a good bar, there's the Spinning Blade, at the edge of town."

He raised both eyebrows.

She held her hands up, laughing nervously. "Oh, don't get me wrong, sir," she said. "It's not a rough sort of place or anything, but they don't serve food, they have music every night and..." she dropped her voice again, "most of the bands aren't on the approved list."

He put a hand to his mouth in mock-horror. "Scandalous," he whispered.

She giggled.

"Thanks for the tip," he said, "but I think the Corner Tavern is more my speed."

"Of course, sir," she nodded, all business again. "I've mapped the route to your Endo. Enjoy your evening."

"You too."

The Corner Tavern was, as promised, a very decent sort of place, done up in faux brick and wood paneling, with subdued lighting and fake plants. It was the sort of place young people took first dates when they wanted somewhere that seemed fancy but didn't have the money to pay for a place that actually was fancy. It was a place for married couples on obligatory date nights who've decided a meal eaten silently under dim lights was preferable to another night watching vids on the couch as it got them out of the house and forced them to wear pants after six. Jase saw both types of couples at the tables, as well as one or two from the second type who'd decided to have a go at being part of the first type again. He decided to leave the tables for the romantically inclined and had his dinner at the bar instead, scrolling through some news feeds and a few comics he followed as he ate.

He was just finishing his meal when a pair of coveralled windfarmers sat down at the bar near him, a man and a woman who both looked to be in their mid-20s.

"Ugh," the man said. "This place again. Let's go to the Blade."

"No," she said. "I'm hungry, and we have work in the morning. I have to be up on sixteen first thing. I'm not doing that hungover, or, since it's you, still drunk."

"Oh, c'mon," he said. "That was one time."

"Yeah," she said, "and that time made me swear it would be the last time." She ordered a beer and one of the specials.

"You better be careful, Di," he said with a smirk, "or you'll be an old woman by the time you're thirty." He ordered a beer and a shot, along with a burger.

"You'd better be careful, Steve," she said, "or you won't actually make it to thirty."

Their drinks arrived, and he toasted her with his shot glass. "To living fast and dying young," he said, downing the shot. He chased it with half his beer, then belched.

"To finding a better class of friends," she said, rolling her eyes. She sipped her beer. "So," she said, "how was your day? I barely saw you at all."

"My day was shit," he said. "I was out overhauling the back twenty all day, and I have to go back out again tomorrow." He finished his beer, and ordered the same again when the bartender delivered their food.

"Overhaul?" she swallowed a mouthful of food. "Shit, man, that sucks."

"Yeah," he said around a mouthful of burger. "That so isn't even my job. Fucking Hollis, man."

Jase's ears perked up at this. He ordered a stim.

"That fucking guy," Di said, shaking her head. "What was he thinking? I heard his indenture was almost up."

"I dunno," Steve said. "He threw away a lot just to stick it in some hillbilly piece of strange."

"You're disgusting," she said.

"What?" he said, shrugging. "She was pretty hot. I don't know that I'd bail on an indenture just to fuck her, but still."

She shook her head, putting her fork down. She took a long pull on her beer. "Honestly, why am I friends with you?"

He downed his second shot and grinned at her. "I assumed it's because you're secretly in love with me."

She made a face. "Ugh," she said. "Not while I'm eating."

"Excuse me," Jase shifted closer to the pair. "Pardon the interruption, but I couldn't help overhearing. You're talking about Jan Hollis?"

Steve glanced over at him, bleary eyes narrowing in suspicion. "Who wants to know?"

Jase smiled and handed over a card. Advanced as modern tech was, the humble calling card still had its place. "Jase Logan. Human Resources."

Steve's eyes widened. "Uhh, listen," he stammered, "I know I was being a bit lewd with Di, but I wasn't harassing her, okay?" He looked over at her. "Right?"

She didn't reply. She had taken the card and was studying Jase.

"Relax," Jase said. "So long as she doesn't file a complaint, you're not my job today. Still," his voice took on a stern tone, "dial it back a little, okay?"

Steve nodded, then swallowed. He took a hasty drink of his beer. "Um, yeah, so, okay," he rambled. "The thing is, I don't think we should talk to you, without, y'know, without our boss or somebody."

Di rolled her eyes. "Oh, for fuck's sake, Steve," she said. Looking at Jase, she said, "What do you want to know, Mr. Logan?"

Jase moved to the open seat next to Di. As he sat down, the bartender brought his stim. He took a sip. "Well now, Di, is it?"

She nodded.

"Well, Di, Steve here isn't entirely wrong. You should have your executive manager, or your foreman, or at least a crew chief present during official questioning," Jase said, slipping into his friendly HR patter. He always liked to lead with friendly HR patter. He also had an HR asshole routine for when the friendly patter wasn't doing the trick, but he always hated pulling that one out. Both HR personas were a slog to maintain. Jase couldn't do asshole or friendly for very long, preferring to spend most of his time slouching around the vicinity of polite disinterest. However, given the urgency of the task, and his situation, he had the feeling polite disinterest wasn't going to get the job done. "That said," he went on, "this isn't official questioning. No one's names are going on any sort of record. I'm just trying to get some background."

"Uh, yeah," Steve said, growing more nervous the longer he was in the presence of HR. "So, then, that means we don't have to talk to you, right?"

"Right," Jase nodded. "We're just chatting, and you're under no obligation to chat with me."

"Right, ok." Steve stood, and his eyes got the unfocused look of someone reading a Endo display. He tapped at the air, paying his bill. When he finished, he said, "I'm going to the Blade." Turning to Jase, he said, "If you want to ask me about Hollis, do it tomorrow when my boss is around."

"Fair enough," Jase said, smiling.

"You coming, Di?"

Di shook her head. "I'm still eating," she said. "Plus, I want to chat a bit."

"Di..."

"Have fun at the Blade," she said. "Tell Lora I said hi."

Steve looked like he wanted to say more, then he just snarled and walked out.

The bartender came and cleared Steve's plate, and Di indicated he could take hers as well. She ordered a stim. "Clear and sweet, please," she said, ordering it without creamer.

The bartender nodded, then glanced meaningfully at Jase. "You ok here, Di?"

"I'm fine, Jim," she said. Then, looking at Jase, she asked, "Right?"

"We're just chatting." Jase grinned at the bartender, who grunted and walked off with the plates. Turning to Di, he asked, "Friend of yours?"

She nodded. "Since grade school," she said.

"You grew up around here?"

Another nod, this time with a smile. "Yeah," she said. "I'm second generation windfarmer. My dad retired a senior foreman."

Jase had surreptitiously called up her employment file and glanced through it. "You're up for crew chief," he said.

"Reading my file?" she raised an eyebrow. "And here I thought we were just chatting."

"Sorry," Jase said, holding up his hands. "You're right."

She waved his concern away. "Read it, if you want. I'm a good worker."

Jase nodded. "You are. So, what made you choose the family business?"

She laughed. "Not much else to do in a company town but work for the company, and I didn't want to work service. Plus, I did really well in school. You know what the schools are like in these towns, right?"

Jase nodded. Schools in company towns geared their curriculum toward training workers for whatever industry the town was built around. Some students would always fall through the cracks of a system like that, but there were places such people could work, if they didn't just leave town.

"So, yeah," she said. "I had an aptitude for it, and the first time my dad took me up on a turbine, that was it." She grinned. "That's what I wanted."

"You're lucky," Jase said. "Not many know what they want so young, and find themselves in a position to do it."

She nodded. "But," she said, "you didn't come over here to talk about me. What can I tell you about Hollis?"

"Anything." Jase shrugged.

"He was a good worker," she said. "I was his shift supervisor a few times, and I noticed he always went above and beyond. Not as surly as most indentures, either." She mused on that a bit. "Of course, he was green badge, so..."

"Yes," Jase said. "His mother needed an expensive surgery. He indentured himself and the company paid for it."

"I'd heard it was something like that," she said. "That makes it even crazier that he deserted. The company could turn around and demand his mother repay the full amount of her surgery."

Jase shook his head. "We won't," he said.

"No?"

"I put in a recommendation to defer any punitive actions pending his reacquisition," Jase said. "Nothing is going to happen to anyone until I find him." He made a mental note to actually put that recommendation in, the next time he spoke to Alen.

"You think you will?" she asked. "Deserters aren't easy to track down."

"It's why I'm here," he said.

They busied themselves with their mugs of stim for a few moments.

"What can you tell me about Moira Townes?" Jase asked, finally.

Di shrugged. "Not much. She showed up about a day or so before Jan split, looking filthy and ratty, y'know, typical refugee trash."

Jase blinked.

"What?" she said, not quite defensively, but not without rancor. "You don't like that I called her trash?"

"I didn't say that."

"You don't have to." She studied him a moment. "You're from the Metro?"

"Born and raised."

"Yeah," she said. "Figures."

"I don't see how--"

"Look," she said, "I get that things are bad in Appalachia, okay? You don't have to tell me how awful the Archers of Christ can be. My dad's parents were Muslim, my mom's a mix of Catholic and Jewish. I heard enough horror stories about the Purges growing up to have a pretty dim view of those people."

"They aren't all like that, Di."

"Yeah," she said. "Well, the ones who aren't should be fighting the ones who are, not coming to decent places looking to suck our tits dry." She shook her head, waving the subject away. "Whatever," she said. "Anyway, poor little refugee Moira came crawling into the farm around late afternoon. We were all waiting for Johns to show up and deal with her --"

"Johns," Jase interrupted her. "That's Van Johns, your executive manager?"

"Yeah," she said, "him. Well, he must have been more hungover than usual that day, because he was nowhere to be found. By then it was around quitting time, and a few of the nastier sort started taking an interest."

Jase nodded. There was more than one of that sort on most energy farms, which was why Steve had been so worried. National Consolidated had developed very strict anti-harassment procedures, and no one, no matter how tough or hardened they thought they were, wanted to run afoul of them.

"Anyway," she said, "that's when Hollis got involved. He fought off two of the bigger assholes, and just when it was looking like someone was going to die, Johns finally showed up. He set Townes up in the onsite indenture dorms, and that was that." She shrugged. "Next day, she and Hollis were gone."

Jase nodded. This matched his official report, for the most part. "Well," he said, "it looks like I'll have plenty to talk to Mr. Johns about when I meet with him tomorrow morning."

Di laughed. "You scheduled a morning meeting with Van Johns?" She rolled her eyes. "Good luck with that. Besides," she said, "he wouldn't tell you shit, anyway. You want to talk to Doris Mahoud, the foreman."

Jase tapped a note into his Endo. "Really?"

"Yeah," she said. "Johns is a prick, and he'll only give you as much as he has to, and even then he'll just cover his own ass. Doris will give you the straight story."

"Thanks," Jase said. The bartender approached, and Jase gestured to the stims. "I've got this."

"Kind of you," Di said, reaching into a pocket on her coveralls, "but I need to pay for my dinner anyway." She pulled out a small device and tapped at the screen.

"Is that a phone?" Jase asked.

"Yeah," she grinned, holding it up before tucking it away.

"Haven't seen one of those in a while."

"Right? Endos are everywhere now. Problem is," she said, "I've got the circuit allergy."

"Oof," Jase said, "that's rough. There's treatment for that, though."

She chuckled. "Not on my med plan." She shrugged. "Phone does the job well enough. Anyway," she said. "I have an early day tomorrow, so I'm off home."

"Have a good night," Jase said, "and thanks for your help."

She nodded. "Good luck," she said. "I hope you find him."

"Me too," Jase said.

CHAPTER 4

The next day, Jase had the car drive him out to the farm before the first shift arrived. The main office was built in the mid-twenty-first century modular architectural style, which meant it looked as though someone had jammed a bunch of cargo carriers together and then grafted a tangle of tanks and pipes and wires to them before finally sticking a small wind turbine or solar panel on top of the whole mess and calling it done. The style had developed in response to the chaos following the First Corporate War. The new American nations were still forming and establishing their borders, so there was very little infrastructure to speak of. Buildings needed to be self-contained and self-sufficient, and no one really cared how pretty they were; they were happy to finally have a place to go where no one was shooting at them anymore. An older woman was unlocking the front door, which was part of a foyer that had clearly been added much later, when the car pulled up.

"Hi!" Jase called up to her as he stepped out of the car. He hopped up the steps two at a time, his hand outstretched. "I'm --"

"You're the HR rep from corporate," she said, looking at his hand, then up at him.

He held his hand out just a beat too long, then slowly brought it up to his head and ran it through his hair. "Um, yes," he said. "Jase Logan."

"Right," she said, opening the door. "Here about the deserter, I expect." She stepped through, letting it close behind her. She didn't quite slam it in his face, but still made it clear she'd be perfectly happy if that happened on its own.

Jase caught the door before it shut, shoving it open and stepping through. "I am," he said, following her through a dingy waiting area to the cramped and equally dingy office. He had the feeling that friendly HR patter wasn't going to cut it, but he was hoping he wouldn't have to go full HR asshole. He brought a bit of authority to his voice. "What do you know about it?"

She busied herself with the usual tasks of opening the office. She disabled a few alarms, turned on lights, and powered up a handful of computers that had been relics when Jase's grandfather was a boy. She flipped a switch on what must have been a first-generation stim brewer, back when they still tried to make it taste like coffee or tea, then sat down at one of the old computers and began typing at the battered keyboard. It was so old and used that the keys were all blank, their numbers and letters worn away. She typed solely from memory.

Jase stood awkwardly, then felt embarrassed about standing there. He tried to assert some control over the situation. "I said --"

"I heard you," she said, "but I need to boot up the farm, or no work is getting done today. So, unless you want to tell corporate that you caused one of their energy farms to lose money by the second..."

He said nothing.

She busied herself at the computer as Jase heard a low rumble building from outside.

"Turbines," she said.

"Yeah," he answered. "It's not my first time on a windfarm." He waited a moment more, then said, "You done putting me in my place, or are you going to drag this out a little longer?"

She smiled up at him. "I figure I'm about done."

"Great. So," he said, "what do you know about Jan Hollis' desertion?"

"Ran off with a girl two nights ago," she said. "Pretty little slip of a thing out of Appalachia." She clucked softly. "Poor dear."

"And that's all you can tell me?"

She shrugged. "That's all I know."

Jase smiled. It was his thin little professional smile, the one he put on when he'd had about enough of someone's bullshit and was warming up his HR asshole routine. He looked around the office, gesturing toward the closed door at the back wall. "That Johns' office?"

She nodded.

"Where is he?"

"Mr. Johns keeps his own hours."

"Does he?" Jase arched an eyebrow. He found it to be an effective companion to the smile. 'Never use your voice for something your face can do on its own' was something old Sumir, the man who'd taught him the ropes, had often said.

She nodded.

Jase paused a moment, letting her return to her work. "What's your name?" he asked suddenly.

"What?" She looked up and blinked.

"Your name?"

"Mariah," she said. "Mariah Steffords."

"Tell me something, Ms. Steffords." He leaned across her desk. He hoped he was looming menacingly. Often when he did this, he worried it just looked like he was trying not to fall over. "While Mr. Johns is off 'keeping his own hours'," he said, "who runs things around here?"

She stared at him.

"So, that would be you." He leaned back, letting his thin little professional smile deepen into a knowing smirk. Friendly HR patter had nearly gotten him a door to the face. Time to see what HR asshole would get him.

"I never said--"

"You don't have to," Jase said. He wandered around the office, stopping in front of an old filing cabinet. He opened a drawer, revealing folders full of papers. Another drawer contained actual disks and tape cartridges. He looked down at the bottom drawer, wondering if it held wax tablets etched in cuneiform. He walked slowly back toward her, noticing that she was watching him. He was dragging this out, partly because that was all part of the routine, but also because he really didn't want to do what he was about to do. He remembered something else Sumir used to say: 'You can't always be the nice guy, kid. Sometimes, you gotta be the asshole. These people see HR, they clam up, thinking we're here to start shit. Sometimes you gotta give 'em a bit of shit, so they give you what you want. It ain't pretty, but it's the job'. Jase had never forgotten that, no matter how much he hated it. He hated the idea of being unemployed, homeless, and stripped of his citizenship even more, so he grit his teeth and got on with it. "So," he said, "I'm guessing Johns doesn't really do much around here, does he?"

She said nothing.

"Now, I'm sure an absent boss is just what you want," he said. "Johns holds the title, and all the hassles and responsibilities that go with it, but you do the actual work. Everyone knows that, from the foreman to crew chiefs and the shift supervisors on down, so you get the authority." He had returned to her desk, and he stood uncomfortably close, staring down at her and trying to ignore the sick feeling in his gut.

She blinked up at him.

"Ms. Steffords," he said, shifting into his stern professional glare and speaking with the clipped professional tone that went with it, "I could not possibly give less of a shit who runs this windfarm, so long as it is run smoothly and efficiently. Based on the records I've seen, it has been." He paused. He was deep into his HR asshole routine now. Sumir would be proud. Just as she was about to speak, he said, "Until one of your indentured workers ran off with some refugee, and corporate had to send me out here to clean up your mess."

"I --"

"So," he said, "I can report back that the executive manager of this windfarm is a drunken layabout, and that daily operations are handled by the office manager." He grinned down at her. "I can also report that you'd done an admirable job, but the pressures were getting a bit more than you could handle." He shrugged. "Johns would be fired, obviously, and you..." he looked down at her. "Well, I guess that would depend." He softened his expression and his tone just enough. "Or," he said, "I can keep all this to myself, and you can stop dicking me around and tell me what you know, which is clearly more than 'he ran off with a girl'." He crossed his arms. "What's it going to be, Ms. Steffords?" He was pleased he was able to do this without visibly shaking.

"Honestly, Mr. Logan," she said, her hands trembling, "that really is all I know. Hollis was a good worker, a hard worker -he'd even made shift supervisor once or twice, and that's rare for an indenture."

It was. Jase was impressed. "That alone would have earned him a nice severance package, a full-time position, or both," he said. "I don't imagine anyone is pretty enough to entice someone away from that."

She shook her head. "I swear to you, Mr. Logan," she said, "I don't know a thing about it. Yes, I pretty much run this place day-to-day. But there's still plenty that's Van's eyes only. A lot goes on behind that door that I don't know about." She gestured toward Johns' office.

"Hm," Jase looked toward it.

Mariah looked down at her hands, which were twisting around themselves in her lap.

"I'm sorry I spoke to you the way I did," Jase said, feeling the deep sickening regret that usually kicked in around this point in the HR asshole routine. He really had no right to play that routine anyway, given that it was likely his fault any of this had even happened in the first place.

She nodded. "I'm sorry I was so rude," she said. "Van..." she sighed. "Mr. Johns has been receiving these calls from corporate. I thought you might be mixed up in that, and I was resentful."

"Calls?" Jase raised an eyebrow.

"Strange ones," she said. "The callers, and it's not always the same caller, won't identify themselves, even though the calls are clearly coming in from the Metro office. I transfer the call through to Mr. Johns, and then the line goes dead."

"Is that strange?"

"I listen in on a lot of his calls," she said. "It helps to keep track of things, especially if he's been..." She waved her hand, her face flushing. "Well..."

"Right," Jase said, nodding.

"But the line goes silent every time he gets one of those corporate calls. Then, afterward, he makes these odd changes to procedures."

"Odd?"

She nodded. "The first change he made was moving the green badge indentures out of the employee housing into the red badge barracks."

"What?!"

"You didn't know?"

Jase shook his head, and the sickening regret rolled around in his gut for a while. He definitely should have known that. He should have been alerted to that. He probably had been, and he'd skimmed the alert without reading it before marking it 'acknowledged' and going back to screwing around.

"To be fair," she said, "he didn't put red and green badges in the same buildings, but still. Indentures aren't supposed to be restricted like that, unless they're red badge."

"No," Jase said, "they absolutely are not." He flicked at the air, and his Endo display registered a wifi signal. It, like everything else in this office, was ancient, but he was able to connect to it. He tapped on the desk, apparently lost in thought, while he was actually sending a data-miner into the windfarm's network.

"Then," she said, "he curtailed their freedom of movement. Said they needed passes from the office to go to town, and then only on weekends."

Jase's eyes widened. "That's..."

"I know."

"Did you report any of this?"

She shook her head. "He told me it came directly from the highest levels of corporate, and if I said anything... well, he said..." she looked awkwardly at him.

Now his face flushed. "He threatened you, much the same way I did."

She nodded. "I was so sure you were part of this, that I was going to be silenced, even though I hadn't said anything! I..." She began to cry. "Please," she sobbed, "this job is all I have."

"Hey," Jase reached out and took her hands in his. "Ms. Steffords..."

"Mariah."

"Mariah." He smiled. "I am so sorry for the way I acted. This case with Hollis is exerting a lot of pressure, and I..." He shook his head. "None of that is any excuse."

She smiled at him, then pulled her hands away and wiped her eyes with a tissue. "Apology accepted, Mr. Logan."

"Jase."

"Jase," she said. "My own behavior didn't make things easy for you."

He smiled again. "Well, then," he said, "I accept your apology, as well." He offered his hand. "Shall we call it even?"

"Works for me," she said. She returned his smile, shaking his hand. "Can I offer you some stim, Jase?"

"Sweet and creamy, please, Mariah."

They were finishing their stim and having a pleasant chat when another woman walked in. She was younger than Mariah, but older than Jase.

"Hey, Mariah," she said. "He stagger in yet?" She jerked a thumb toward Johns' door.

"Of course not," Mariah answered. "Oh, Doris," she said, gesturing toward Jase, "this is Mr. Jase Logan, from corporate HR. Jase," she said, "meet our foreman, Ms. Doris Mahoud."

Jase stood, and Doris looked him over. She glanced over at Mariah, who nodded. Smiling, she held out her hand. "Nice to meet you, Mr. Logan."

"Likewise, Ms. Mahoud," Jase said. "I hear the two of you pretty much run this place."

"More or less," Doris eyed him warily, glancing again at Mariah. "Johns still handles most of the big stuff."

"So I understand," Jase said. "Still," he said, "I was wondering if we could talk."

Doris shrugged. "Fine by me. I need to give the farm a quick once-over before first shift, so if you don't mind riding along, we can talk as we go."

"That works," he said. "Lead the way."

"So," Doris said, "you're here about Hollis." She was driving a small electric cart out into the rows of turbines. The sound their blades made as they moved through the air combined with the cart's low electric hum created an interesting and not unpleasant white noise. Jase sat in the passenger seat of the cart, and Doris' gear was piled on the broad seat behind them.

"Yes," he said, "though I've since learned a few things that have expanded the scope of my visit." He was hoping his data-miner would lead to some answers, and that Ms. Mahoud would provide even more.

"You heard about the new rules?" She turned sharply down a path between two rows of turbines.

"Yes," he said.

"She tell you the latest?" The cart began to slow, and she looked around.

"About the passes?" he followed her gaze, noticing people curled up on the ground against the bases of the turbines. They seemed to be wrapped in blankets and sleeping bags. A few had set up simple lean-tos that opened against the turbines. "What..?"

"I'll explain in a minute," she said, getting out of the cart.

"Did they sleep there?"

"Yeah. Just a sec." She walked toward the sleeping people, and gently woke them. They gathered around her, and she passed around what looked like business cards made of hard plastic to each of them. She walked back to the cart. When they were underway, she said, "So, yeah, they sleep there."

"It's early spring," Jase said. "It still gets pretty cold at night, especially out here."

She nodded. "It does. That's why they sleep up next to the turbines."

He raised an eyebrow.

She chuckled. "Don't you know how these things work?" She gestured toward the metal towers with their spinning blades.

"I know the basics," he said.

"Yeah, well, if all they did was generate power, they'd be pretty useless. There's still not much in the way of international infrastructure."

"Huh," he thought. "That's a good point."

"There's a reason National is so invested in energy production, and that they do so much of it out here." She pointed to the base of one of the turbines. "There's a battery in there, a proprietary design from National. It's the highest storage capacity and lowest amount of leakage of any battery ever made. Once it's charged, someone comes by and swaps it out for a spent one, then the charged one is sent out to any number of places. The solar farms have them too."

"How much power can you get from one of those?"

"A small neighborhood," she said. "They'll power the average skyscraper too, or one of the larger factories."

"From one battery?"

She nodded.

"Huh."

"Anyway," she said, "the bases of these things get pretty hot, so they make for good places to sleep for those that don't have better places."

"Who are they?" he gestured toward another group of sleepers they were approaching.

She shrugged. "People fall through the cracks in the corporate towns. There's only so much work to be had, even here. Plus," she said, "when you've got a whole workforce you don't have to pay, it doesn't make much sense to hire from town." She stopped, got out of the cart, and repeated the interaction from earlier. Jase would see her do it three more times before they returned to the office.

When they were moving again, Jase asked, "What are those things you're giving them?"

"Day chips," she explained. "They're for day laborers. Gets them access to the cafeteria, the showers, the laundry facilities. They can use them to get food and such in town." She shrugged. "Hell, I'd hire most of them as day laborers, if I could. But..."

"The indentures."

"Right. So, I figure the chips are just sitting there, may as well do some good with them. I'd give them better places to sleep, but I can't get away with that, so I let them sleep near the turbines and come by in the mornings before first shift so no one else finds them." She looked at him out the corner of her eye. "This could get me in a lot of trouble."

He shook his head. "Not from me."

She nodded. "So," she said, as they drove on, "back to Hollis and Johns' bullshit with the indentures."

"Please."

"The weekend passes aren't the latest thing," she said. "The latest thing is the suspension of those passes."

"What?"

"Yeah," she said. "About a week ago, Johns suspended all weekend passes for indentures. Now they're stuck here on the farm." She shook her head. "I don't know what that refugee girl told Hollis, but it must have made life on the run seem better than whatever is going on here. Honestly," she said, "I'm surprised more haven't followed him."

Jase turned away, watching the turbines slide past. "So am I."

CHAPTER 5

Jase returned to his hotel having never spoken with Van Johns, the infamous executive manager who was apparently still sleeping off a binge somewhere. It didn't matter. Between Mariah Steffords, Doris Mahoud, and the results of his data-miner, Jase had all the relevant information he was likely to get from the windfarm's offices. He used the hotel's direct connection to the corporate network to upload the data, a preliminary report, and his Endo recordings of his conversations with the two women. He omitted any scenes of Doris' charity toward the homeless townspeople, not wanting her to face any repercussions from the company. He also made a compressed and encrypted copy of everything, which he uploaded to one of his numerous data storage accounts via one of the public networks available through the signal drones. The references to corporate were making him nervous, so he also ran a history wipe on the upload, preventing a network trace. Once everything was where it needed to be, he pinged Alen directly.

"Hey hey!" the other man's voice sounded in Jase's head. "How's our man on the ground?"

"Intrigued," Jase said, grinning. "Take a quick look at the files I sent up. Skip the video, I'll summarize, but give the datafile a once-over."

"Ok, hang on." There was a click, and Jase was on hold. A few moments later, and Alen was back online. "Holy shit," he said.

"Yeah," Jase said. He then gave Alen a brief summary of his conversations with Doris and Mariah.

"What the fuck?" was Alen's response.

"Right?" Jase shook his head. "I mean, ok, it's pretty obvious why Hollis left now..."

"You think?"

Jase chuckled. "But this opens up a whole..."

"Yeah."

"I mean, those calls were executive encryption."

"I know."

"That means..."

"It does."

Jase and Alen sat quietly on the line for a while. Finally, Alen spoke.

"Okay," he said, "let's run it down. We've got encrypted calls from someone at the EVP level or higher to the windfarm..."

"Yup," Jase nodded.

"We have a steady erosion of any and all indenture rights..."

"Apparently."

"Then this refugee girl appears out of nowhere, and we get our first desertion in almost a decade."

"Right."

"We'd be stupid not to think it's all connected."

"That we would," Jase agreed. "Still," he said, "I can't see how Townes could possibly be connected. I mean, she has to be a coincidence, right? She showed up, and Hollis took advantage of the opportunity."

"Maybe," Alen said. "Awfully convenient timing, though."

"Yeah," Jase said. "That's what I was thinking."

"Still," Alen said, "we don't have enough data to connect her to anything, so let's call her a coincidence for now."

"Sure."

"Anyway," Alen said, "what now?"

"Well," Jase said, "my guess is they headed south, to El Norte."

"Not a bad guess. They don't have extradition with any of the other nations or corporations. Hollis could hide out there for the rest of his life."

"Yeah, but I don't know if that's his plan," Jase said. "There's still his mother. He was willing to indenture himself to pay for her med care. He's not going to just bail on her now."

"So... what, then?"

Jase thought. "Cascadia, maybe? IRISCorp is headquartered there, and they're none too friendly with National."

"Fair point," Alen said. "What's your next move?"

"I'm not sure," Jase said. "I'm going to poke around town, see if anyone saw them leave. It's a slim chance, but I'll take it. Then, I'll probably head south. Check out the El Norte theory."

"Be careful down there," Alen said. "Republica del Norte is outside our citizenship jurisdiction."

"Right," Jase said. "Okay, so, if I find anything else, I'll ping you."

"Sounds good."

"Oh," Jase said, "also, put a hold on any punitive measures toward Hollis' mother."

"Already done."

"Good man." Jase smiled. "And I want to fivestar Mariah Steffords and Doris Mahoud."

"Fivestar?" Alen was surprised. "That's going to --"

"They deserve the bump in salary, and the bonuses, believe me."

"Okay then," Alen said. "Consider it done."

"Thanks, man."

"You got it, bud. Be safe."

"Yes, Mom."

"Fuck you."

"Dick."

The call ended, and Jase made his way back down to the lobby. The concierge offered to call a car, but Jase decided to walk. It was a nice day, and he wanted to see some of the town. He was therefore a bit surprised to see a car waiting for him. It was a black luxury sedan, though it clearly had more than a few miles on it, for all that someone had very recently tried to clean it up. He should have seen that as his first warning.

The next warning should have been the driver. Like the car, he had more mileage on him than he wanted to show. He was dressed well, in a black suit that was just a little too worn to be truly professional. The driver was smiling, and if Jase had been paying attention, he would have noticed that the smile was forced, and never made it anywhere near his eyes.

"Mr. Logan," the driver said, "so glad I caught you." He opened the back door of the car. "Please."

"No thanks," Jase said. "I'll walk to town."

"Are you sure, sir?" The smile slipped, revealing a look that made Jase take a step back.

"Uh, yeah," Jase said. "Yeah, I'm good, thanks."

The driver sighed, and suddenly, there was a gun in Jase's face. "Please get in the car, 'sir'," he said, all pretense of a smile gone, "or some poor bastard is going to have to mop your brains off the sidewalk."

"Uhhh..." Jase had always imagined that, should he ever find himself in such a position, he'd face it with a bit more steely-eyed resolve, possibly with a quip or two, delivered in the low growly voice his father used when he was angry about something, but didn't want to make the effort to yell about it. As it happened, Jase just stood there with his mouth half-open, dizzy and more than a little queasy.

"Get in the fucking car," the driver hissed, stepping forward and grabbing Jase's arm.

Jase had always wanted to learn kung-fu, which, to his mind, had the best moves for disarming the unlucky bastard who'd ever dare shove a gun in his face. He'd never actually managed it, of course. It wouldn't have mattered if he had, since his legs had gone so wobbly as to barely hold him up, let alone be capable of the jumping spin kicks Jase had always assumed would be brilliant at a time like this.

Therefore, rather than flip-kicking his assailant down the sidewalk, Jase essentially fell into the back seat of the car, winding up in the lap of another man. He was hard to see, but he shoved Jase off him as the door slammed shut. Jase heard the muted taps of the driver's shoes on asphalt, and it was only once the car had started and was pulling away that Jase realized he'd had that brief moment to try to escape.

"You've been looking into things you shouldn't, Mr. Logan," the other man said from the shadows of the back seat, "and sharing information that you should have left alone. We think it's best you disappear for a while, let things settle down."

"Wh-where are you taking me?"

The man smiled, and Jase wished he hadn't.

"You'll find out."

Something hard and heavy slammed into the left side of Jase's head. Gray fuzzy spots danced and swirled around his eyes. The something hard and heavy hit him again. The gray fuzzy spots merged into a swirling gray mass, he heard a rushing sound in his ears, then everything went black.

Jase drifted in and out of consciousness. He heard the low rumbling of the car, felt the cool tackiness of old imitation leather against his cheek, and smelled that uniquely unpleasant smell that only a very old car acquires, along with the greasy scent of a biodiesel engine. There was another smell, too, also unpleasant. It was familiar, but he couldn't place it. He knew music was playing, but it wasn't loud enough and he wasn't conscious enough to make it out. He also heard bits and pieces of conversation, though he couldn't follow a lot of it.

"Town still there?" That was the man beside him.

"Looks like no," the driver said. "I mean, it's still there, but ain't no one around."

"Heard she hit it last week."

"Guess so."

"This is bad."

"Yep."

"Should tell Gunnar."

"Gunnar knows."

Jase drifted out again.

When he came to, they were talking again, or maybe still talking.

"...should kill him."

Panic tried to fight its way through the thick fog around Jase's brain. They had to be talking about him!

"Gunnar says no," the driver said. "Says she'll come for him."

Or maybe they weren't.

"Yeah," the man in back said, "and when she does, we toss her his head then put a bullet in hers."

"Not how Gunnar wants to do it."

Jase felt like he should know who this 'Gunnar' was. The name was very familiar, and it gave him a low-grade awful feeling. Unfortunately, the part of his brain that held most of his actual knowledge didn't seem ready to wake up yet.

"How I would do it," the man in back said.

"Oh yeah?" the driver laughed. "You want me to tell him that?"

"Fuck you."

"Tell you what," the driver was clearly taunting the man in back, "soon as we're back, I'll tell Gunnar you know better how to run things. Let's see how that goes."

"Fuck you!" The man in back was getting agitated. "Shit, man! I was just talking."

The driver laughed.

"How much longer?" The man in back was surly now. "I think this asshole pissed himself."

That was the other smell, the one Jase couldn't identify. He didn't think it came from him, though. He didn't feel wet.

"Nah," the driver said. "Had an old dog back there for a while."

Jase felt oddly proud he hadn't wet his pants.

"Shit, man," the man in back said. "Clean your fucking car once in awhile."

"I do clean my car, asshole," the driver said. "You know how hard it is to get the smell of piss out of carpet?"

"Whatever."

Jase drifted again.

When he came back around, he could hear rain hitting the car. He was also starting to notice a headache and a stinging pain around his left eye that throbbed in time with his pulse.

"...such shitholes," the driver was saying. "I mean, look at this fucking road! It's barely there!"

Jase was forced to agree. The constant bouncing and shaking of the car wasn't doing his head any favors.

"Kinda the point, isn't it?" the man in back said. "These places were fit to live in, we wouldn't be able to do our thing."

"I guess," the driver said.

They were silent a while.

"Hey," the driver said at last, "you hear he wants to hit Knoxville?"

"What?" the man in back laughed. "Is he crazy?"

"Don't let him hear you say that."

"Yeah, fine," the man in back said. "Just between us, does he honestly think he's got a chance against one of the city-states? Shit, we're still digging out from that mess in Birmingham."

"He thinks we can take it."

"I think he's starting to buy into his own bullshit."

"You want to tell him that?"

Jase could almost hear the man in back roll his eyes. "Christ," he said, "will you give it a fucking rest?"

"Hey, that's blasphemy," the driver said.

"Oh, fuck you."

Jase drifted off again.

He woke two more times, once briefly, in the car -the men were fighting, but Jase couldn't follow it at all- then for good when the car stopped. He was drawn up roughly and a bag went over his head. It was stiff in places and smelled vaguely of copper. When they pulled him out of the car, he heard gravel crunch under his feet, and felt raindrops on his skin. There was an overpowering smell of coal in the air. It made him slightly ill, but he swallowed the feeling back down. He was pretty sure if he threw up in the bag, they'd make him keep it on. The cold rain was actually helping.

He was dragged from the car into a building. The rain stopped, and the coal smell wasn't as bad, but he could hear people talking and moving and working all around him, which was disorienting. It was also a bit colder inside, and he felt chilled in his wet clothes. Before he'd even gotten his bearings, he was dragged away. As the sounds of people receded behind him, he could hear the echo of two pairs of shoes on the floor, along with his own shuffling steps. He guessed he was being dragged down a hallway.

He was jerked to a stop. He heard a door open, then was dragged forward and shoved into a chair. He heard a door close and assumed he'd been locked in a room. It was warmer than the rest of the building, and the light coming through the bag was softer. A new voice spoke from in front of Jase.

"This him?"

"Yes, sir," the driver said, his voice much more deferential. Jase assumed he must be sitting with the infamous 'Gunnar.' He still thought he should know that name. He hoped the part of his brain that knew things would wake up at some point. He had a feeling someone was going to expect him to know things very soon, and that it would not go well for him if he didn't.

"Take the bag off him," Gunnar said.

The bag came off and Jase blinked, grateful it hadn't been removed out in the more brightly-lit hallway. He looked around as his eyes got used to the light.

Randomly spaced lamps gave a soft warm glow, reflecting off gleaming wood surfaces, and illuminating row upon row of books. Bookshelves of all sizes and styles covered the walls. Any space not covered by books displayed an eclectic collection of artwork. A comfortable couch nestled between two shelves, an elegant coffee table in front of it. It could have been mistaken for a professor's office or someone's den, if not for the flag.

A large red flag hung over the couch. In the center of the flag was a white circle, and inside the circle was a black cross. Two bundles of arrows formed a blue 'X' behind the circle/cross symbol. Jase had seen the flag of the Archers of Christ on the news feeds often enough; it was something else seeing it in person.

The sudden realization that he'd been kidnapped by the most notorious terrorist organization in the American nations also helped him remember who 'Gunnar' was. Jase looked around again. The part of his brain that knew things was wide awake now, but all the things it knew were awful.

"Oh, shit," Jase said, before he could stop himself.

The man behind the desk laughed. "You're not the first man sitting in that chair to say that," he said. "But yeah, I am who you think I am." He offered his hand. "Gunnar McReady," he said. "I'm the leader of the Archers of Christ."

CHAPTER 6

Jase hurriedly shook Gunnar McReady's hand, realizing that this was not a man to offend. He looked around again, absently noticing his kidnappers were still in the room. He recognized the driver from his thin, wiry frame and ratty suit, as well as the cruel gleam in his eyes. The man Jase identified as the one who had been sitting with him in the back seat was much larger. He was broad across his shoulders, with thick, meaty arms, and doughy about the middle.

Gunnar McReady, on the other hand, was tall and lean, without an ounce of body mass wasted on fat. He kept his graying hair cut short, and was clean-shaven. Between his hard physique, the eyes that shone with a cruel intelligence, and the network of scars crossing his body, Gunnar McReady looked like he'd seen his share of fighting.

In fact, Jase thought, Gunnar McReady looked like he'd seen more than his own share of fighting. He looked like he'd seen about ten people's share of fighting, and was still in the mood for whatever fighting anyone had laying around.

"Ok," Gunnar said to the others, "you two can go. Give me and our guest a bit of privacy."

The two men nodded, offered a couple of muttered 'yes sirs', and left, closing the door behind them.

After a moment of looking Jase over, Gunnar asked, "So, you doing okay? Looks like you got a decent clip 'round the head."

Jase reached up and touched his head where he'd been struck. He still had a headache, and the throbbing in his head was worse. He winced as his fingers made contact with a sizable lump.

"Yeah," Gunnar said, wincing in sympathy. "Sorry my boys were so rough with you. You should get some ice on it."

"I-I'll be ok," Jase said. His voice was thick and raspy, and it occurred to him that he was incredibly thirsty.

Gunnar chuckled, getting up from behind the desk. "Relax," he said. "I'm not going to kill you for needing an ice pack." He opened a small refrigerator, one of the newer models, taking out an ice pack and a bottle of water. He handed the pack to Jase, who gingerly placed it against the side of his head. Gunnar then put the water down in front of Jase on the desk. He went back to his chair and gestured to the water. "You sound thirsty," he said. "Don't worry. I'm not going to drug you or poison you. Here." He reached across and screwed off the top, making the audible crack of a seal being broken, and then put the bottle back on the desk. He sat back and smiled. His smile reached his eyes and was quite friendly, but Jase was pretty sure it was for show. Still, he picked up the bottle and took a long pull, keeping the ice pack pressed against this head.

"Thank you," he said.

"Sure thing," Gunnar said, still smiling. "Feeling a bit better?"

Jase nodded as well as he could. "Much."

"Good. So, let's get to it." He pointed at Jase. "Jase Logan, right?"

"Yes."

"Yeah." He shook his head. "So, Jase..." he raised an eyebrow. "Can I call you Jase?"

"Please." Jase didn't think friendly patter or his asshole routine were going to get him very far. Well, the HR asshole routine would probably get him as far as an unmarked grave in the woods, but he wasn't in a big hurry to find out. That usually left polite disinterest, but he had a sinking feeling he would be expected to show some interest in what was being said. He opted for just being polite.

"Great. So, Jase, here's the thing." He folded his hands on the desk. "You've been looking for this deserter, what's his name..." He waved his hand absently. "Hollis... something..."

"Jan Hollis." Jase decided that when sitting across from the leader of the most feared terrorist organization in the American nations, it was probably a good idea to be helpful. He hoped polite and helpful would be enough to get him out of this, as he didn't have much else to offer. A few jokes, maybe, but he didn't think they'd go over.

Gunnar snapped his fingers, pointing at Jase. "Jan Hollis! Yes! That guy." He shrugged. "I could give a fuck about that guy, but, here's what I do care about Jase..." He leaned across the desk. "I care very much about getting Moira Townes back."

"Wh-why?" Jase didn't think he should be asking questions, but it just slipped out. He realized then that, in addition to polite and helpful, he could also offer complete idiocy. He wasn't sure how far that would get him, and made a mental note to maybe not try so hard to find out.

Gunnar smiled and sat back in his chair, steepling his hands. "Well now, that's an excellent question," he said, in a tone of voice that suggested he would give Jase that one, but it would be a very good idea if he didn't ask any others. "See," he said, "I don't really need *Moira* back; I just need what she stole from me." His smile became decidedly less friendly. "I *want* her back so I can explain to her, very carefully, exactly what happens to people who steal from me."

Jase made a point of not asking what Moira Townes had stolen from Gunnar.

"So, what I want you to do, Jase," Gunnar said, "is, when you find your deserter, if Townes is with him, you drop her here on your way back to the farm."

"Oh, um, sure, yeah," Jase stammered. "I can totally... totally do that. I just, uh, that is..." He realized, just a hair too late, that he was about to ask a question, that thing he was pretty sure he was supposed to stop doing.

"Why you?" Gunnar grinned. It was a grin that said he was going to let this second question pass, because he liked Jase, but the next one might be answered with a bullet in his head.

"Well..."

"Nah, it's a good question. I got plenty of people could track her down. Thing is, though" he leaned in close, as though imparting a secret "I'm not really liking the direction this little investigation of yours is taking, so I thought I'd get you back on track."

"Um, but I was--"

"Yeah, you were heading down south, gonna check out El Norte," Gunnar said. Jase was less shocked than he should have been at the idea of McReady being aware of his encrypted communications. "Not a bad idea," Gunnar said, "and once we've had our little visit, that's what I think you should do. Hell, we'll give you a lift to the border. But Jase..." he shook his head, "you really have to keep your eye on the prize, okay? Stop poking around in things that don't concern you, yeah?"

Jase nodded.

"Great!" Gunnar clapped his hands together. "I knew you just needed a bit of a talking-to. And don't worry," he said, "your buddy up north is getting one too, probably as we speak."

Jase wasn't about to ask who was giving Alen the talking-to, though he hoped Alen's was a bit more professional than his. He had a feeling he already knew the answer, and was certain it would be one question too many.

"Okay, then," Gunnar said, standing. "Just one thing left to do." He went to the door and knocked. Two large men entered, one of them pushing a gurney. "That's him," he said, pointing to Jase. "Make it quick, and try not to fuck him up too much."

"Wh-what..." Jase dropped the ice pack and tried to get out of his chair, banging his knee on the desk and spilling what was left in the water bottle. He was grabbed by one of the men, who threw him down on the gurney. Gunnar came to stand over him.

"Well, you see, Jase," he said, "you seem really cool about this now, here in my office, with all my boys around, and you thinking you're gonna get shot if you say no, but I'm worried that once you're free and clear, you might not think so much about seeing Ms. Townes back home."

Jase was strapped to the gurney.

"So, I'm gonna need some insurance."

CHAPTER 7

J ase woke up to find he was lying on a cot. It was a nice cot, all things considered. It had a proper mattress on it, for one thing. Also, it wasn't a cold metal table with thick straps and a bearded lunatic wielding a knife and a pair of pliers. That was where Jase had fallen asleep.

To be fair, he hadn't so much fallen asleep as passed out. He remembered being strapped down to the table, and the bearded lunatic starting to carve his Endo out of his arm, dock and all. He'd wanted to make a joke about voiding his warranty, but only managed to scream in agony and vomit all over himself before passing out. He looked down at his arm, which was throbbing in time with the pounding in his head. He noticed that someone had made a cursory attempt at cleaning him up, though the smell of his own sick was now a disgusting counterpoint to the sour proof that he needed a shower. A bloody bandage was wrapped around the site of his Endo. His fingers twitched in response to random pulses in his haptic sensors, and he felt stinging shocks up and down his arm into his head. It was as though he were getting a tattoo directly on the nerves of his arm, with an electrified needle, by a blind artist who may also have been drunk. His Endo display flickered and pixelated in his field of vision, causing a painful strobing effect in his eyes. He flicked his fingers to close the display, but it took several tries before it worked. He closed his eyes with a weary sigh and wondered what they'd done to him.

"A bomb, most like," a voice said from above him.

Jase looked up with a start, then winced at the myriad shocks of pain that simple motion caused.

A gaunt-looking older man, who was somehow oddly familiar, smiled kindly at Jase. He held up his hands. "Hey now, son," he said. "I'm a friend."

"Y-yeah?" Jase rasped. "Cause I gotta say, no one's been very friendly since I got here."

The older man laughed. "I hear that," he said. "They beat me up something terrible when I arrived." Jase could see a purple bruise around the man's left eye. He also had what looked like a few days growth of beard on his face, greasy white hair, and an outfit not much cleaner than what Jase had on. Jase was thankful no one else was around, given that their combined smells could probably kill a horse.

"You're..." Jase's voice was little more than a whisper, "You're a p-prisoner... too?"

The man looked down at him, a look of sympathy on his face. "Yeah, hang on," he said. "We'll get back to introductions in a minute." He came near the bed, slowly, and very gently lifted the head of the cot, so Jase was supported in a seated position. Then the man went away, toward a small kitchen area in what Jase could now see was a trailer of some kind. Jase heard the sound of a refrigerator being opened, then the man came back with a bottle of water. He made a show of breaking the seal, then handed the open bottle to Jase.

Jase drank most of the bottle down, then handed it back. "That's twice someone's felt the need to prove they aren't trying to drug or poison me," he said. "That has to be a bad sign."

The man smiled. "Well, it probably isn't good, no," he said. Then he held out his hand. "John," he said, "John Sunderland."

Jase's eyes widened. He knew why this man looked so familiar. "From The Sundowners?"

John laughed. "Man, you remember that?"

"You were my favorite band. Hell," he shrugged, grimacing again at how much it hurt, "you're still in my top five. Oh." He remembered his manners. "Jase Logan." He shook John's hand.

"A pleasure, Jase," John said. "Always fun meeting a fan, even after all these years."

"So, um, I have to ask..."

"What in the world am I doing here?" John laughed again. It was an easy laugh, as was his smile.

Jase grinned.

"Well," John said, "that kinda goes back a ways. After The Sundowners broke up... okay, first, you know I'm a Christian, right?"

Jase nodded. "I always thought you were more spiritual than religious, though," he said. "Your faith came out in your songs, but they were never preachy."

John smiled and nodded. "Thank you," he said. "That's what I was going for. Anyway," he continued his story, "after we called it quits, I decided I wanted to make an even deeper commitment to Christ, so I got myself ordained."

"You're a..." Jase sought the right word. "...priest?"

John smiled. "You're thinking of the Catholics," he said. "No, I'm technically a minister, but really more of a preacher."

Jase nodded.

"I figured I had been given this gift of music, and I'd made a pretty good living off of it for a while, so maybe it was time to use that gift in service to the Lord," John said. "I started up a traveling ministry that, if I may say, has become rather popular throughout the Confederacy, parts of the Midland Republic, and several Appalachian city-states."

"Wow," Jase said. "We never heard about any of that up north."

"I imagine not," John said. "Christians aren't too popular outside the southern nations."

"Hey," Jase said, "that's not entirely true. The Commonwealth still has a fairly sizable Christian population, and you find a lot of Catholics in the Metro."

"You know what I mean," John said. "If I recall, they tend toward an almost secular Christianity in the Commonwealth, and Catholics have always been their own special breed of cat. I'm a bit more the evangelical sort these days, though I hope I'm still not too preachy. My wife says I go on a bit, but then she's always busting my chops." He smiled.

"Fair point," Jase said. "The Archers haven't done Christianity many favors up north or out west."

John shook his head. "They're not doing it many favors down here, either." He sighed. "You know where they came from?"

"They grew out of some weird sect from the pre-Split days, right?"

"A few of them," John said, "not to mention various white supremacist groups, and other such hate mongering organizations."

"Ah."

"Yeah," John said. "Now, even back before the Split, or the Crash, or the Peak, or whatever 'good old days' you want to dredge up, it was pretty hard times around here. Mix in those sects that encouraged their followers to have as many kids as possible, and those times became a lot harder. If you weren't lucky enough to let folks gawk at you on the TV, money wasn't easy to come by. After the Split..." He spread his hands. "Well, by then, you had a few generations of a lot of these movements. Generation after generation of families having as many kids as they could, generation after generation of hate and bigotry... By the First Corporate War, you had a great many people with a whole lot of anger, looking for a place to put it." He paused, then asked, "What do you know about that War?"

Jase shrugged. "Not much. My knowledge of history begins and ends with what we learned in school, and since I went to a corporate school, history class tended to gloss over both Wars."

"Well, some say the War happened after the Split, some say it caused it. Truth is, both happened around the same time. So, we had these United States, right?"

"Sure."

"And the United States were pretty powerful, even by that time, when most of their power was based on posturing more than anything else. They had soldiers all around the world, getting themselves involved in all manner of other people's business. So," John said, "as things got more and more contentious here at home, they weren't getting any less so out there. Money was tight, since the government pretty much only taxed the poor at that point, and it was getting harder to support a full military. It was considered much cheaper to just outsource most of their foreign adventurism to some military contractor or other."

"Right," Jase said. "I heard about that. The War started as a bidding war, right?"

"Pretty much." John nodded. "That devolved fairly quickly into fighting over territory. Eventually, they gave up any pretense of working for the US government and just started carving out little fiefdoms for themselves." His face twisted into a grim smile. "Wasn't long before they realized what worked over there could probably work just as well over here. A few of the larger corporations got into the act, putting resources behind the different military contractors, and they had themselves a big old game of war with this country as the board. This region and the inner cities were favored battlefields. They tried to avoid fighting in places where people still had money.

"Anyway," John said, "a new movement grew up around this area during the worst of the fighting, focusing on that passage from Isaiah: 'He has made My mouth like a sharp sword, In the shadow of His hand He has concealed Me; And He has also made Me a select arrow, He has hidden Me in His quiver'. This new movement, I forget the name of it, started calling on young men to be 'as arrows in the quiver of God'."

"Oh," realization dawned on Jase.

"Yeah," John said. "That war was Hell on Earth, especially around here. Even before the War, or the Split, Appalachia was just barely hanging on in parts, especially out in the country. When the War blew through... well..." He shrugged. "That was it. It was then that some patriarch or other looked around at his family, and others like it, saw that his nearest and dearest were living on the edge of ruin, some with nothing to eat and nowhere to live, and he thought maybe it was about time some of those arrows came out of God's quiver and into His bow. And he figured maybe God was leaving it to him and his to draw the string."

"The Archers of Christ."

"There you have it."

"What about McReady?" Jase asked. "He doesn't seem terribly devout."

"He isn't," John shook his head. "When something like the Archers reaches this size, and lasts this long, it opens itself up to... hm... let's call it 'outside influence'. Gunnar is ex-militia. He fought for National Consolidated in the Second Corporate War. Most of the higher-ups in the Archers of Christ are all Corporate veterans, and none of them are terribly devout, either. The rank and file still are, though."

"But how can they follow someone like McReady, who isn't ...?"

"He can play the role when he needs to," John said. "He also puts a roof over their heads, food in their bellies, and provides them someone to blame for their troubles. That goes a long way."

"Yeah," Jase nodded, a wave of grief passing across his face. "I know it does."

"You alright, son?"

Jase waved his hand. "Old wounds," he said. "Not important."

"I would disagree," John said, "but if they're old, I don't want to open them up. You got enough fresh ones as it is."

Jase grinned.

"Still," John said, "you want to talk..."

Jase nodded, then changed the subject. "So, you still haven't told me why you're here."

"Right!" John said. "Right, right. Well, to make a long story short," he said, "I'm here as bait."

"Bait?"

"For my wife."

Jase blinked. "Your wife?" he asked. "Why would the Archers care about..." he recalled a conversation overheard in the car.

"You ever hear the name Amanda Halford?" John asked.

Jase's eyes grew wide. "You're married to the leader of the Parish Coven?"

John smiled. "I am, indeed."

"Huh." Jase thought about that a moment. "From what I hear, they've had more luck than anyone fighting the Archers."

"That they have," John said, no small amount of pride in his voice. "McReady's hoping that by kidnapping me, he can lead my fiery Wiccan priestess into a trap."

"Wait," Jase said. "Back up. How--"

"How did a Christian preacher end up married to a Wiccan priestess?" John laughed. "It's a bit of a tale."

"We have time."

"You'd think so, right?" John shook his head, chuckling.

"What's that supposed to mean?"

"My lady's no dummy, Jase," John said. "She won't spring McReady's trap, but she'll spring me, and I'll make sure you come along too. I imagine that's going to happen sooner rather than later."

"Like, right now?" Jase looked toward the door, as though expecting it to be blown off its hinges, which honestly wouldn't have surprised him in the least. It had been that kind of day.

John smiled. "Well, no."

"So, time for a story, then."

"You seem awfully eager to hear it."

"I'm awfully eager to be distracted from the throbbing pain I'm feeling all over my body, and the fact that, apparently, my left arm might explode at any moment," Jase said.

"Fair enough," John said. "Well, the thing about this story is, Amanda and I have told it so many times, we actually put it to music."

"She's a musician, too?"

John nodded. "She's a fair hand at the bass guitar, and has a beautiful voice. Her true passion is committing horrific acts of violence against the wicked, however, so she doesn't really practice as much as she should. Still, someday we'll sing you the song we wrote.

But," he said, "I suppose for now I can give you the abridged version."

Jase settled back against the pillow, sipping his water.

"Let's see," John said. "This was, oh, ten years ago now, give or take. I'd just begun my ministry, and her coven was little more than a traveling grungepunk band that did a bit of light vigilantism on the side. We were playing a festival in one of the Confederate city-states..."

"Wait," Jase said. "An actual coven, playing grungepunk at a festival in the Confederacy?"

John laughed. "I know," he said. "You think they'd be run out on a rail. But this was Athens, which is one of the semi-autonomous city-states. They're a bit less strict about some of the laws and mores the Confederacy lays down."

Jase nodded. "I've heard," he said. "It's kept quiet, but it's pretty well-known the Confederate government doesn't control its territory with all that much of an iron fist."

"They do in lots of places," John said, "just not that one. Well," he amended, sadly, "not then, anyway. Now..." He sighed. "Athens changed after the last siege, and not for the better. But," he said abruptly, his mood changing, "that's not my story. Now, while it's true places like Athens and Savannah and even Birmingham have been a bit more open and welcoming of those that don't fit the..." He cleared his throat. "Let's call it the 'desired model' of Confederate citizen, not everyone felt so charitable. Plus, agents of the Archers, and other, lesser-known groups, were everywhere in those days, stirring up trouble. So," he said, "there I was, having just finished my set, a whole album's worth of songs about God's love and the virtue of tolerance and acceptance, when I was set upon backstage by a group of... well" he smiled ruefully "they weren't fans, I'll tell you that. They jumped me, busted up my favorite guitar, and set to beating on me something fierce. They would have beat me to death if Amanda and her bandmates hadn't come along." He shook his head. "Now, I'm a 'turn the other cheek' sort of Christian, Jase, always have been, but I'm not ashamed to say I took no small amount of pleasure watching those boys get the walloping they deserved."

"What happened to you?" Jase asked.

"Ah, those ladies took me in, patched me up, even bought me a new guitar," John said. "I was a while recovering, and Amanda's the best medic of the crew, so we spent a fair bit of time together. We got to talking, once my head was back on straight, and we found that, disparity of our faiths aside, we hold to similar values. Plus, we like a lot of the same music and share a sense of humor."

"The cornerstone of any relationship," Jase smiled.

"Indeed," John said. "So," he continued, "we joined up together, traveled the highways and byways of the Confederacy, even up into the Midland Republic a bit; she sang her Threefold Law, I sang the Word of God, and we both worked as best we could to do right by those who'd been done wrong. Amanda coined the term 'Parish Coven', and we decided to make it a true interfaith ministry." He smiled, his eyes losing focus as he looked back through time. "A few years into all that, we were married."

"Any kids?"

John shook his head. "Neither God nor her Goddess saw fit to bless us with a child, mightily though we tried," he said. "Eventually, we decided our mission was more important."

"It *is* quite a mission," Jase said. "How do you reconcile your faith with hers?"

"Easily," John said. "I don't consider them at odds."

Jase raised an eyebrow.

John sat back and looked Jase over. "Are you a religious man, Jase?" he asked.

Jase shook his head. "Not really. I believe there's some higher power out there, but I don't believe anyone truly knows what it is."

John smiled. "On that, we wholeheartedly agree."

"Say again?"

John chuckled. "It occurred to me, a very long time ago, that if God is truly omniscient, omnipotent, and omnipresent as we say, then a being like that would be too far beyond us to ever understand, even the tiniest bit. That's where religion comes in, and that's why I don't hold with the notion that one is any better than the others."

"How so?"

"You ever look at an eclipse?"

Jase was slightly taken aback by the non-sequitur. "Um... no? I thought you weren't supposed to look directly at them."

John smiled and nodded. "Exactly. Looking directly at the eclipse can burn out your eyes, so you need to use one of those little boxes. They project the eclipse onto their interior, making it safe to look at. That's all religion is, a little projector box that allows us to safely experience the Divine. Once I started seeing it that way, it was easy to acknowledge that I didn't have the only box. Maybe the other boxes are different from mine, but we're all looking at the same eclipse."

"Huh." Jase was thoughtful. "That's a great way of thinking of it."

"Thank you," John smiled. "Honestly, it's the work that's important. Ideally, the Parish Coven Interfaith Ministry is meant to provide refuge and seek justice for the downtrodden."

"But?" Jase prompted. "It seems like there's a 'but' in there."

"But," John said, "while Amanda and her crew have been dealing out justice, we haven't been able to provide as much refuge as I'd like."

"Why not?"

"Money, for one," John said. "Sheltering and feeding people tends to require a lot of it. Plus there's the matter of our fugitive status. Hard to set up a refuge for the less fortunate when you're on the run from a notorious terror organization." He thought a bit and grinned at Jase. "Mostly though, it's money."

Jase nodded. "It usually is. Still," he said, "it really does sound like a worthwhile mission."

"Thank you," John said. "You know" he flashed a grin "there's always room for another stout heart and keen mind on that mission."

"How do you know I have either," Jase asked, "let alone both?"

"I can tell."

"Yeah, well." Jase glanced down at his lap. "I don't know about that. Besides, I'm on a mission of my own, such as it is. I should probably see it through." He looked up at John. "I'm not always so great at that, at seeing things through, so I figure I should start with this."

John nodded. "And there's the bomb." He pointed at Jase's arm.

"Right," Jase said, lifting his arm and eyeing it as though it were ticking, like a bomb from an old cartoon. "Thank God you reminded me. It would be a shame to..." He yawned "To forget that."

"Here." John took the water bottle. "I think we've jawed enough for one night. You've got quite a bit of healing to do, bomb or no, and I've never found a better cure than rest."

Jase nodded, smiling his thanks as John lowered the cot gently down to a flat position. "Thanks, John," he said, yawning again. "I wouldn't say I'm enjoying this experience, but you've made it less horrible than it could have been."

"My pleasure Jase. You sleep well, now."

"G'night, John."

"Good night, Jase."

CHAPTER 8

L ater, when recounting this story, Jase was never sure if it was the sound of the explosions or the shaking of the trailer that woke him. All he knew in the moment was that he woke from a deep sleep to all hell breaking loose outside. He had no idea what was going on, and said as much when Gunnar McReady burst into the trailer.

"What's going on?!" McReady grabbed Jase by his shirt, hauling him out of bed. Everything that had hurt the night before still hurt in the morning, with the added encumbrance of an overwhelming stiffness in every muscle of his body. He let out an involuntary cry, desperately trying not to shed any tears in front of his captor. McReady had lost his air of cool menace, and was in the grip of something closer to panic. Jase wasn't sure if panic was more frightening than cool menace, but he was pretty sure panic was more likely to get him killed at the moment.

"I have no idea!" Jase yelled over the deafening explosions. His head still throbbed in time with his arm, and he could feel those tingling bursts of pain up and down his left side as the compromised Endo caused his internal circuitry to misfire. The flickering display was back as well, and he had to struggle to clear it. This did no favors for his headache.

McReady looked around. "Where the fuck is Sunderland?!"

Jase also looked around. "I don't know!" The explosions were getting louder and closer. Jase could also hear screams. Amid all the fear and the pain, Jase's heart sank a little. John had been rescued, but he hadn't taken Jase. Jase wasn't angry -John didn't owe him anything- but now he was trapped here with an unhinged psychopath and no way out.

"Bullshit! What the fuck is this?" McReady gestured toward the door. "Did you two cook this up?!"

"What?!" Jase laughed. A small part of him suggested that might not be the best idea.

That part of him was right. McReady snarled and punched Jase, who fell to his knees and rubbed his jaw. A different small part of him remarked that at least his injuries weren't all on the same side of his body anymore.

"Don't you fucking laugh at me!" McReady pulled a gun, and Jase found himself staring down the barrel.

"Hey, I'm sorry!" Jase put his hands up, but stayed on his knees. "I shouldn't have laughed, but come on! I don't know anything! He was here when I went to sleep!"

"So when did he leave?!" The gun was shaking. "Did he set this up?!"

"I said I don't know!" Jase yelled. "I just woke up when you got here!"

McReady laughed, a short bark with little humor in it. "Oh, right!" he shouted. "You just *happened* to wake up *now*?!"

Jase was getting annoyed, either in spite of the gun and the incessant explosions or because of them. "It's MORNING!" he screamed.

The explosions suddenly fell silent. Through the ringing in his ears, Jase could hear the moans and cries of the wounded.

"Right?" he asked quietly, looking around, then up at McReady. The gun was no longer pointed at Jase.

McReady's gun arm had dropped to his side as he listened carefully and he held up his other hand. "Shh!" he said. "Hear that?"

Jase could barely hear McReady through the ringing in his ears. He concentrated, and, despite the ringing, he heard, or rather felt, a low rumbling. It was getting louder, which made Jase think whatever was making it was getting closer. "What is that?"

"Tank," McReady said. "Or tanks." A look of furious concentration crossed his face. He shook his head. "Shit."

"What?"

"Shut up."

Jase shut up.

Then an amplified woman's voice called from outside. "Gunnar McReady! This is Colonel Ela

Kincaid of the Midland Militia! Your soldiers are dead or dying, and we have secured your base! There are non-combatants here! Give yourself up, and no one else needs to get hurt!"

McReady shook his head, slowly at first, as though trying to clear it, then with greater fury. "No no no," he said, beginning to punch the wall in time with his words. "No no no no NO! This was not supposed to go down this way!" He turned away from the wall. Jase saw blood dripping from his knuckles. "The militia?!" He seemed to be railing at someone who wasn't there. "You called the fucking militia?! You were supposed to come get him yourself!"

Realization dawned on Jase. This was all Amanda Halford's doing. She hadn't fallen for McReady's trap, just as John had said. But, also as John had said, she'd managed to spring it anyway. Unfortunately for McReady, this made the trap blow up in his face. Unfortunately for Jase, he was stuck in a trailer with a mad terrorist whose trap had just blown up in his face. McReady turned and saw him, as though for the first time.

"You," he said, pointing with the gun. "Get up."

Jase rose -with no small amount of difficulty- to his feet. McReady grabbed him and put the gun to his head.

"Okay then," he said. "They want to fuck around, I can fuck around. Open the door."

Jase opened the door. Early morning sunlight streamed in, causing him to squint as McReady dragged him outside. When his vision cleared, he saw that the trailer was surrounded by armed soldiers. Two tanks aimed their guns at them. A woman was seated half-in and half-out of one of the tanks, a microphone in her hand.

The corpses of men littered the ground, many of them little more than shredded hunks of bone and meat. The Archers of Christ didn't allow women soldiers, so all the women were huddled together with the children, encircled by militia soldiers. Another group of men, women, and children, had been gathered together. They were all dressed in rags, filthy, and half-starved. They'd been given blankets, and medics were tending to them.

"Tell your people to stand down, Colonel!" McReady shouted. "Or I put a bullet in his brain!" Jase felt McReady's hand tighten on his arm, and the barrel of the gun press against his temple.

There was a tense and very uncomfortable silence. Finally, a loud click was heard, followed by a brief whine of feedback.

"I don't know who that is," Colonel Kincaid said through speakers mounted on the tank.

McReady opened his mouth, then closed it. Jase felt a horrible sensation in his stomach. He was glad he hadn't eaten much in the past couple of days. His pants were filthy as it was.

"He's..." McReady shoved the gun even harder against Jase's temple. "He's my hostage!"

"No, I get that," Colonel Kincaid said. "My point is, I don't know him, so why should I care if you shoot him?"

The feeling in his stomach got much worse, and as his head went light, Jase said a silent prayer to whomever was listening that he not faint.

"He's an innocent civilian!" McReady shouted. "You're supposed to care on principle!"

"What's his name?"

"Jase Logan!"

"Why is he here?"

"I kidnapped him!"

"Why?"

"None of your business, that's why!" McReady yelled. "The point is: he's my prisoner, and I'll kill him if you don't let me go!"

A hush had fallen over the compound as everyone watched in fascination. Even the wounded were quiet, as though not wanting to disturb the moment with their moaning and crying, and, in some cases, dying. The microphone clicked on again, echoing across the small clearing.

"No, look," Colonel Kincaid said, "I'm sorry, but, the life of some random civilian isn't worth letting you go." She looked at Jase, smiling sympathetically. "I really am very sorry."

Jase waved his hands weakly. He attempted to say something on the subject of the relative value of human life, the burdens of command, and the necessity of sacrificing the one in favor of the many, but all that came out was, "Aghn."

Suddenly, there was a loud crack. The prisoners screamed, and several of the children began crying. The pain in Jase's head increased, and his first thought was that he'd been shot. He then thought it would have hurt more, being shot in the head, followed closely by the thought that he probably wouldn't be capable of this much thinking if he'd been shot in the head, and also McReady wasn't holding his arm anymore. Only then did he turn and look down to see McReady's corpse, with half of his head blown away. Jase had a hazy realization that the lumpy stain on the door of the trailer was probably the missing part of McReady's head.

"Well, it's about time," Colonel Kincaid said, testily.

Jase turned around to see her looking over her shoulder. "Honestly," she said. "How much longer was I supposed to sit here and stall? I was this close to show tunes and pub trivia, I honestly was."

"I --" Jase said. An odd blackness was creeping in around the edges of the clearing. He wondered if anyone else noticed.

Colonel Kincaid turned back around. "Ah," she said, smiling. "Mr. Logan. So sorry about that. Never intended you to be hurt, we just needed to... Mr. Logan?"

The blackness was beginning to just cover everything now. He was amazed no one was reacting to it. It really was quite striking. He opened his mouth to tell them about it, but suddenly forgot how words worked.

"Oh dear." He heard Colonel Kincaid's voice from very far away as the blackness overwhelmed everything. "Someone try to catch him before he... oh, never mind. There he goes."

Jase's brain decided this was all just a bit too much first thing in the morning, particularly in light of the past few days, especially with no breakfast, or even a decent cup of stim, so it was just going to shut down and go back to sleep for a while, if the rest of the body didn't mind. The rest of Jase's body tried its best to inform the brain that, actually, it did mind, given that it was currently standing at the top of a flight of steps and tumbling down those steps would not do it, or the brain, very many favors. The brain made it clear it was willing to risk it and was shutting down anyway, at which point the legs announced that they could no longer work under these conditions and slid out from under Jase in protest. Fortunately, the brain had finished shutting down by then and everything went mercifully black before Jase hit the ground.

CHAPTER 9

It had been three days since Jase woke up in what looked like an old military base. It actually looked like an old office building that had once been repurposed into a military base, and was now a place that no one really knew what to do with, but still wanted to keep for some reason.

The first thing Jase had done upon waking was take a shower. Never in his life had a shower ever felt that good, and he hoped he'd never be in a position where he'd need one that badly again. After showering for so long the water turned cold, Jase was given a change of clothes to replace the ratty and filthy suit he'd been wearing. The coveralls were comfortable, if a bit frayed at the cuffs, and the military-style boots fit better than he would have expected. He was also glad for the opportunity to shave. His beard was moving from stubble to scruff, and he wanted to get rid of it before it reached the itchy stage.

Once he'd cleaned himself up and had his bandage changed, he'd begun to pay more attention to where he actually was. Everything was old, from the furniture to the technology. The furniture had clearly been well-made and top-of-the-line in its day, but as its day had passed a very long time ago, everything was looking more than a little shabby. His Endo couldn't get a signal, but that could have been the result of the Archers' meddling. He was starting to get used to the stinging pains in his arm, and his headache was actually feeling a bit better, but the twitching in his fingers was really annoying, and the strobing effect of his display was no less irritating. He doubted he would have been able to do much with his Endo, even if he'd found a signal.

The odd thing was, he also couldn't find any other means of contact with the outside world. He would have settled for an ancient computer terminal, so long as someone had been around to teach him how to use it, but there didn't seem to be one of those either. The most modern technology in the entire place was an actual working DVD player and a television that looked like it had been built by cavemen.

He couldn't get a straight answer from anyone about where he was. All they would tell him was that he was in the Midland Republic, under military guard. He wasn't a prisoner, but, for his own protection, he couldn't leave the building. No one would tell him what he was being protected from, either. Since no one seemed terribly interested in him beyond keeping him inside, and he apparently had free run of the place, he'd contented himself with exploring.

Unfortunately, there wasn't really that much to explore, and he'd seen all that was worth seeing in a day or so. He'd figured out the DVD player and TV, but most of the movies available didn't interest him. There were a few superhero movies from the early 21st Century, but the effects were so horrible he couldn't even sit through the first five minutes of one before shutting the whole mess down. Eventually, he decided to just read in the library, which had a pretty decent collection of books, for all that they were printed on actual paper. He was in the library making his way through a battered copy of some horrid supernatural romance or other, when someone finally came to speak with him.

He was brought to an old conference room. Upon entering, he could see where bars and restraints had once been added to make it an interrogation room during the building's tenure as a military base. Apparently someone had decided they didn't need all that at some point and tore them out. A uniformed woman who looked vaguely familiar stood. Another woman, dressed in a dark suit, remained seated, frantically rummaging through a briefcase.

"Mr. Logan," the uniformed woman said, "my name is Colonel Ela Kincaid of the Midland Militia. We met briefly at the Archers' compound." She smiled. "Given the circumstances, I wasn't sure if you'd remember me."

"Yes," he said. "I remember now. You were there, in the tank, with the..." He mimed talking into a microphone.

"Yes," she said. "I apologize again for all that."

"Not at all," he said. "I get it." He held out his hand. "A pleasure to meet you properly."

She shook it, smiling again. "Likewise, Mr. Logan." She turned to the woman seated next to her, who was still searching through her briefcase. Her search was becoming less frantic, as it was becoming increasingly apparent that whatever she was searching for was not going to suddenly turn up on her fifth rummage through one of the inner pockets. "This is Agent Parker," Colonel Kincaid said, "of the Midland Investigations Bureau."

Agent Parker looked up, forcing a smile through a lingering panic. "Oh, uh, yes," she said. "Hi." She held out her hand. "Um, yes. Hi. Agent Kay Parker. A, uh, pleasure."

Jase shook her hand, smiling. "Nice to meet you."

"Shall we sit?" Colonel Kincaid said, with a sidelong glance at Agent Parker.

They sat. Colonel Kincaid grabbed a bottle of water from the center of the table, indicating Jase should help himself. He did.

"So," Colonel Kincaid said, "I imagine you're wondering what you're doing here."

"I *was* curious," Jase said.

"You're not a prisoner."

"That's what everyone keeps telling me."

"You just can't leave the building."

"They tell me that too."

"It's for your own protection."

"And that."

Agent Parker chose that moment to abandon her search, tossing her briefcase on the floor and looking over at Jase.

"Jase," she said amiably, grabbing a bottle of water, "can I call you Jase?"

"Sure."

She took a sip of water. "So, tell me Jase, how's your arm?"

"You mean this one?" Jase held up his left arm. The wound around his Endo had been cleaned and the bandage replaced once a day since he arrived. "It hurts, to be honest. A dull throbbing pain around the dock. Also, I get these weird tingling shocks running through the circuitry to my head, which, thanks to getting knocked around by McReady and his goons, also hurts. The flickering strobe effect any time my display opens, entirely at random intervals, whether I want it to or not, doesn't help," he added.

"I'm sure," Agent Parker smiled. "So, you know what the Archers did, right?"

"My, uh, cellmate," Jase didn't feel like bringing John's name into this, "told me it was probably a bomb."

"Oh, it's definitely a bomb," Agent Parker said, "along with a tracker, and a bug for any comm use. What did McReady want from you?"

Jase gave them a brief summary of Hollis' desertion, the windfarm, and Moira Townes. He then told them what McReady wanted him to do.

Agent Parker nodded. "Yeah," she said. "Then, the tracker and bug were to make sure you stayed on-task, and the bomb was just in case you didn't." She thought a moment. "I'm going to want to talk to you about everything you learned on the farm, and anything else you may have seen or heard in the Archers' compound."

"Okay," Jase said. "I'm happy to help, but none of this really explains why I'm here, or why I can't even go outside."

"The thing is, Jase," Colonel Kincaid said, "even though McReady is dead, there are other Archer cells out there and we don't know who he told about you. Until we finish cleaning up those cells, anyone could have the means to track you, listen in, or even set off the bomb. With that in mind," she said, "we brought you here."

"To the Museum of Obsolete Media?" Jase asked.

"No," Colonel Kincaid said. "We brought you to the last functioning Faraday Base."

"But that was good," Agent Parker laughed.

Jase's eyes widened. "I'm in a Faraday Base?"

Faraday Bases had been built during the worst fighting of the First Corporate War. They were screened against any and all electronic signals, without even a hardline data connection to the outside world. They made great places to plan strategy and store sensitive data, and their locations had been known only to a select few. They made terrible places, Jase determined, to be stuck in for anyone who also had an appreciation for technology or entertainment produced after dinosaurs roamed the Earth. Not many Faraday Bases were still intact and functioning, but those that were had been occupied by the governments of the nations in which they were located.

"Right," Jase looked at his arm. "Makes sense."

"We also aren't sure what might happen if we try to remove it," Agent Parker said. "There's a concern that removing it might set off the bomb."

"Yeah," Jase said, suddenly unable to take his eyes off his arm. "Good call."

"But don't worry," Colonel Kincaid said, "you won't have to live here forever. We put a call out to IRISCorp. They're sending someone immediately."

"Really?"

"Yes," Agent Parker said. "Once we explained the situation, they were very eager to help." She looked at him strangely. "Especially once they heard it was you."

Jase blinked. "Why would they care if it was me?"

"We were hoping you could explain that," Colonel Kincaid said.

Jase shrugged, a confused look on his face.

"Hm," Colonel Kincaid said. "Well, anyway, I have most of what I need. Agent Parker," she looked over at the woman next to her, "I expect you'll share any further information with us?"

"Of course, Colonel."

"Very good." The colonel stood, about to take her leave, when she glanced down at the discarded briefcase. "Okay, look," she said. "I have to know." She raised an eyebrow toward Agent Parker. "What were you looking for?"

The agent blushed, an embarrassed grin on her face. "Oh," she said, "um, well, the thing is..." She sighed. "I'm not used to paper. I mean, who uses paper anymore, right? I'm used to having this" she held up her arm, displaying an Endo that was a generation out of date "tell me whatever I need to know. But, since this is a Faraday Base, I knew I would need to bring a physical copy of anything I needed. I *thought* I had printed out his file."

"But you didn't?"

Agent Parker shook her head.

"So, what *did* you print out?" the colonel asked the agent.

Agent Parker flushed an even deeper red, casting her eyes down. "I'd, uh, I'd... rather not say."

Colonel Kincaid arched her left eyebrow. "Oh, now you have to tell us." She gestured toward Jase, who nodded.

Agent Parker's head fell onto her crossed arms. She sat this way for a moment. Then, with a quick laugh and a long sigh, she reached down and pulled a sheaf of papers from her briefcase. She tossed them on the table.

Colonel Kincaid scooped them up and began reading. As she read, her left eyebrow climbed higher up her forehead. Finally, she looked down at the mortified agent. "Who the hell is Detective Rian?"

Jase blinked, then smiled. "Detective Rian?" he asked. He held out his hand. "Colonel?"

Colonel Kincaid handed him the papers.

He skimmed over them, every so often glancing up at Agent Parker, whose face remained a deep shade of red as she tried to fold herself into her seat.

"This..." Jase said, with a chuckle. "This is *Vampire Detective* fan fiction." He smiled at Agent Parker. "You like *Vampire Detective*?"

"Of course," she said. "Who doesn't?"

"I have no idea what that is," Colonel Kincaid said.

"It's a weekly adventure serial," Jase explained.

The colonel looked from Jase to Agent Parker, her expression growing ever more incredulous. "Are you kidding me?" she finally said.

Agent Parker threw her hands up. "Hey, like I said, I'm not used to paper! I printed the wrong file!" She grabbed the papers roughly out of Jase's hand and shoved them back in the briefcase. "Just tell me when the firing squad is."

"Hey, hang on," Jase said. "I thought it was really good."

"Oh, stop."

"No, seriously," Jase said. "Can I read the rest? I love *Vampire Detective*."

Jase noticed Agent Parker work to hide a delighted smile. "You really want to read the rest?" she asked.

"If that's okay."

Agent Parker grinned, then brought the papers back out and handed them to him. "I'm still working on it," she said, "so it's not finished."

Jase nodded. "Oh hey," he said, "do you watch *Electrospeedster*?"

"Of course!" Agent Parker nodded. "I watch all of them. *Electrospeedster*, *The Hooded Archer*, *Omniwoman*, *Tempus Fugitive*..."

"Oh man," Jase said. "Did you catch the big crossover?"

"That was awesome!" Agent Parker said. "When Rian and Omniwoman were trapped in the Time Vault, and he had to feed on her to survive..."

"But her alien blood gave him that weird virus," Jase said, "and --"

"Yes, well," Colonel Kincaid said, rolling her eyes. "This is all very fascinating, but some of us are actual adults with jobs. And by some of us, I mean just me, apparently." She nodded to both of them. "Mr. Logan, Agent Parker. I'll leave you to..." she gestured toward the pile of papers, "whatever this is." Jase and the agent said their goodbyes, and the colonel left them alone in the room. Once she was gone, the two of them looked at one another, then down at the papers, then back at each other, finally bursting with laughter. They laughed for quite a long time.

"Ohhh," Jase said, wiping his eyes, "oh, that was good. Made my head hurt, but I needed a good laugh." He looked back down at the papers, then back up at Agent Parker. He flipped the corners of the papers with his thumb, then looked up at her. "You didn't bring this by accident," he said.

She smiled, shaking her head. "No," she said. "Your file's up here." She tapped the side of her head.

"This is in my file?" Jase rested his hand on the papers.

"What," she said, "the fact that you love adventure serials? Yeah," she nodded. "That's in there."

"So, this was just some kind of ice-breaker?"

"It was," she said, "but that actually is genuine *Vampire Detective* fan-fiction, written by me, so don't start questioning my fandom bona-fides."

He held up his hands, smiling. "Wouldn't dream of it, Agent Parker."

"Kay," she said, returning the smile.

"Kay." He fidgeted with the papers a bit more. "So," he said, "what else is in my file?"

"Lots of things," Kay said. "One in particular that I'd like to talk about is probably going to be quite painful."

His face fell. "I'm not talking about the Riot."

"I'm sorry, Jase," she said, "but I need to talk to you about the Riot. Look, I know how you feel --"

"Bullshit," he said. "You can't possibly know how I feel. What the hell does some spy from the Midland Republic know about the Riot, anyway?"

Kay shook her head. "I don't know what it's like to lose a child, Jase," she said, "but I know what it was like for you to lose your husband."

"Yeah?" Jase wouldn't look at her. "How would you know that? Am I going to hear some sad story about a dead grandparent, or something?"

"No," she said, and the harsh pain in her voice made him look at her. "My girlfriend died in the September Riot," she said. "So, no, Jase, you aren't the only one to lose the love of your life to a bigoted mob." She grit her teeth. "That one horrible day led me here, to the Midlands, and the Investigations Bureau. Ever since that day, I've been hunting for the ones behind the Riot."

"No one was behind it," Jase said. "It was just a bunch of angry bigots."

She sneered at him through wet eyes. "Grow up, Jase," she said. "Someone is always behind something like that. After five years of searching, I found out who."

"Who?" No sooner was the question out of his mouth, then he felt that horrible twisting in his stomach.

"The Archers of Christ," she said. "Call it a latter-day Purge."

He looked down at his bandaged arm, his jaw clenching.

"The thing is, Jase," she said, a more gentle tone in her voice, "I know there's also someone behind *them*." She looked imploringly into his eyes when he looked up at her. "And I need you to help me bring them down."

CHAPTER 10

"**R**on."

"And... Erin?"

"Our daughter, yes," Jase said, the ghost of a smile on his lips. His eyes unfocused, and he looked back to a much happier time. "When she... uhh..." His voice shuddered, and his eyes became wet. "When... when they..." He grit his teeth, forcing the words out, "When they died" he let out a long breath "it was the end of the happiest time in my life."

"Tell me about them."

"Ron was..." Jase laughed a little. "Oh, it's so tempting to call him perfect, you know? Five years on, all I want to see are the perfect parts of him." He sighed. "And so much of him was perfect. He was smart, funny, kind... he was so good to me, so... supportive. Even when..." He paused. "*Especially* when I came out as transgender." He stopped again, looking at her. "Is *that* in my file?" he asked. "Because I spent a great deal of money, time, and effort making sure it wouldn't be."

She shook her head. "Your marriage to Ron is in there, but there are no records relating to gender identity. I'm impressed, Jase," she said. "You were very thorough. All the way back to your birth certificate. You even managed to seal all of your medical and school records."

"Yeah, well," Jase said, "that was important to me. Not because I'm ashamed of who or what I am, but because I wanted this to be information *I* controlled. I wanted the freedom to choose who I shared this with, and I didn't want it to be something any random asshole could find in a database somewhere. I also..." He sighed and looked past Kay, trying to find the right words. "I also needed to not just *be* Jase, but to have always *been* Jase." He grit his teeth. It had been a long time since he'd had to explain any of this, and he thought he'd never have to do it again. A small voice in the back of his head pointed out that he'd been the one to bring it up. He told the voice to fuck off and looked at Kay, forcing a smile. "I struggled with being Jase for a very long time," he said. "Once I knew, once I finally said it out loud... I knew I *had* always been who I am now, that the person everyone thought I was... that person wasn't a lie, per se, but Jase is the truth, and I wanted that truth reflected back throughout my history."

"I understand."

"Do you?"

Kay shook her head. "Okay, maybe I don't, not in the way you mean, but it makes sense."

"Right," Jase said. "Sorry for being so... intense. This is not a pleasant subject for me." He laughed and wiped his eyes. "It's a painful subject nested inside another painful subject, and one I probably could have left alone, but..." He shrugged. "But we're talking about Ron, and I can't talk about Ron without talking about this. He supported me through every step of my transition: the hormone implant, the surgeries, the whole legal process... He was right there with me, no matter what. So much of that legal process, especially changing my records to the degree they were changed, was all him. He made so much of it possible."

"Was it hard for him, your transition?"

Jase smiled, shaking his head. "If it was, he never let on."

"And Erin?"

Jase shook his head. "I started transitioning when she was barely a year old."

"So she was your natural daughter."

Jase's jaw clenched, and his leg started bouncing. He looked down and away, rubbing his hands on his pants. He was seated in one of the worn leather armchairs in the library. Kay was across from him, sipping a cup of stim. His own cup sat on the table next to him, untouched.

"Jase?" She sat forward in her chair. "Are you okay?"

Jase nodded. "She was my natural daughter," he said, the words rushing out. "I came out shortly after she was born, and yes, the pregnancy and birth were a big part of my finally coming out, and no, I don't want to talk about any of that."

"Of course," Kay said, nodding, a sympathetic look on her face. "I'm so sorry. I didn't think..."

Jase shook his head. "It's fine. Let's just move on." He took a sip of stim, his hands shaking enough to nearly spill it on himself. "I think I've said all I'm going to say about that part of my life."

"Okay."

"I should mention, though," Jase said with a small smile, "that you are the first person I've even so much as thought about sharing any of that with. So, y'know, feel special."

Kay smiled back. "Oh, I do, Mr. Logan."

After a moment, Jase continued his story. "Anyway, yes. We were happy. Blissfully happy. Again, I'm tempted to think of him, of both of them, honestly, as perfect, but of course they weren't. Erin was a child, and, sweet and wonderful as she was, kids can sometimes be annoying little pains in the ass." He smiled ruefully. "What I wouldn't give, though," he said softly, "to be annoyed by that little pain in the ass, just one more time." He wiped his eyes and looked up. "Anyway, Ron would sometimes get in these solitary moods, where he'd just go off and..." He smiled, remembering. "He built models," he said. "Planes, cars, train sets, whole cities... they were incredibly complex, and he was really good at it. But sometimes, especially when he had a lot on his mind, he would just disappear into his workroom for hours at a time, sometimes whole days." He shook his head. "It was really annoying."

"Why did he do it?"

"Ron was always a bit of an introvert," Jase said. "He needed a lot of down time, away from people, to recharge his batteries, so to speak."

"I'm a bit like that myself," Kay said.

Jase nodded. "And I got that," he said, "but, you know, sometimes it felt..." He shook his head. "Doesn't matter. I'm not going to sit here and rehash an old argument with my dead husband."

"So those times weren't perfect," Kay said.

"Right," Jase said. "Except for all the ways in which they were."

"Yeah," Kay said. "So, the Riot."

Jase nodded. "The Riot." He smiled. "God, but that was supposed to be such a great day. Games, rides, music... There was even going to be a-- "

"A giant waterpark, ten blocks by five blocks," Kay said.

Jase nodded. "Erin was so looking forward to that."

Kay smiled. "So were we," she said. "Nora and I loved waterparks."

"Nora was..."

"My girlfriend, yeah," Kay said. "We'd been living together almost six years. She wanted to get married, but I..." She shook her head. "I didn't want to settle down."

"Why not?"

"I was young," she said. "Still in my twenties, still having fun..." She gave a harsh laugh. "I knew I only wanted her and no one else," she said. "That wasn't the issue. It was just that, I was worried if we got married, that would be the end of the fun, you know? The party would be over, and we'd have to settle down, buy a house and raise kids or something."

"And that was a bad thing?"

"It was for me," she said. "I... I really liked to party back then." Her face turned introspective. "It wasn't until after... everything that I realized how desperately Nora wanted the party to be over. She was done. She wanted to grow up, and she wanted me to grow up with her."

"So," Jase said, "the Riot."

Kay sighed. "The Riot." She looked at Jase. "How did you survive?" she asked. "Everyone who was at the Festival died in the Riot, so I assume you weren't there."

"I'd been called into work early that morning," he said. "I told Ron to take Erin and I would meet them as soon as I got out. I was actually on my way, when..."

"When it happened."

"Yeah."

"Well," Kay said, her face a mask of self-recrimination, "I was home, in bed, when it happened. I didn't even know that it had happened until late afternoon."

"Why were you in-- "

"Hangover," Kay said. "We'd gone out the night before, because of course we had. I drank too much, because of course I did, and the next morning, Nora got up early as we'd planned, but I was too hungover to even get out of bed. She was so mad. She..." Kay stopped and looked at Jase. "What were your last words, to Erin and Ron?"

Jase blinked. He hadn't expected that question. "Ron..." He thought a moment. "I sent Ron a video as I was leaving work. Told him I was on my way and I would see him soon. I told him I loved him, and I hoped Erin wasn't eating too much junk." He smiled. "Ron always indulged her with that stuff, especially on special occasions."

"And Erin?"

Jase sighed. "She never heard my last words to her," he said. "She was asleep, and I snuck into her room before I left for work that morning. I watched her sleep for a moment -I used to love watching her sleep- then I kissed her on the head and said, 'Papa loves you, little pumpkin. Have fun with Daddy and I'll see you soon as I can.'"

Kay nodded. "You know what my last words to Nora were?" She wiped tears from her eyes. "She was angry with me, because I was such a drunk asshole party girl I couldn't even get out of bed to go do the thing we'd been looking forward to for weeks, and she was yelling at me. I was hungover, and her yelling wasn't really doing me any favors. So, the very last thing I ever said to the love of my life, during the very last time I would ever see her, was, 'Fuck off, you stupid bitch, and leave me the fuck alone.'" Her voice hitched, and she wiped more tears from her eyes.

"Oh, hey..." Jase reached out for her.

"No," Kay shook her head, holding up her hand. "No, it's okay. Just..." She drew a deep, shuddering breath. "Just gimme a sec."

Jase looked around, found a box of tissues on a side table, and offered them to Kay. She took one and Jase made a detailed study of the mug his stim was in before drinking it very deliberately while examining the patterns the sunlight was making on the wall.

Kay wiped her eyes, blew her nose, and took another deep breath. "Okay. Okay, I'm good. So," she said, "Nora stormed out of the apartment, went to the Festival without me, and by the time I'd slept off my hangover, she had died alone, surrounded by a mob of people who hated her."

Jase nodded. He wasn't really sure what to say, or if he should say anything.

"I changed my name after that," Kay said. "My name was Kay Sherman, but after that, I changed my last name to Parker. That was Nora's name. She'd wanted to marry me, and... and I..." She shrugged and looked down at the tissue she was twisting in her hands. "I thought if I took her name, it would be like we'd gotten married. I thought, 'Okay, so, Kay Sherman was a spoiled party girl who didn't appreciate what she had.

Let's see who Kay Parker is. I bet she's better.' And I knew," she looked up at Jase. "I knew this wasn't just some spontaneous hate mob out of nowhere. Someone was behind it. Someone took Nora from me, and I was going to make sure I took everything from them."

"Is that when you became..."

"An agent?" she nodded. "Yeah. I moved to the Midland Republic and enrolled in the Bureau's academy program."

"Why the Midlands?"

Kay shrugged. "I grew up in the Commonwealth, spent most of my adult life in the Metro, and I wanted a fresh start. Cascadia was a bit of a haul, so I settled on the Midlands. I was a few years in training and even when I got out, I still had to take the missions I was given. Many of them had nothing to do with the Archers or terrorism or any of that, but I never stopped working toward justice for Nora. At some point, I landed a case that dovetailed with my crusade, which led to another case, and then another, each of them setting me on a trail that I eventually followed straight to the Archers of Christ," she said. She paused a moment, then continued. "The thing is, they were behind the Riot, yeah, but someone's been behind them for a while. That's my real target."

"And who's behind the Archers?"

"Well," she said, "that's why your investigation is so important." She offered him a very sympathetic look. "I think National Consolidated has been bankrolling the Archers of Christ since the Second Corporate War, and I think they were directly responsible for the September Riot."

CHAPTER 11

"No," Jase said. He shook his head, sinking back into the chair. He stood up suddenly and paced the room, still shaking his head. "No," he said. "That's insane. They sponsored the Festival."

The full name of the Festival had been 'The New York Metro Diversity Festival', and was being held on the anniversary of the worst of the Purges. The Purges happened before, during, and after the First Corporate War, had been carried out by an assortment of hate groups and terrorists, and had targeted, among others, members of the LGBT community. The hatred these various terrorist groups had felt toward marginalized communities had been building for decades, if not centuries, nurtured from one generation to the next, often abetted and exacerbated by those in power. These groups, of which the Archers of Christ were just one, took advantage of the breakdown in law and order in the years around the First Corporate War to wage their own war on anyone who wasn't cisgender, heterosexual, white, and at least nominally Christian. Millions died in the Purges, and in some American nations, certain populations were eliminated completely. The wounds of those years left deep scars, none of which were even close to healing a hundred years on. Most nations, with one or two notable exceptions, adopted rigorous anti-hate legislation into their constitutions, and all the major corporations made such policies a mandatory part of their culture, at least publicly. The September Riot, along with other, less publicized outbursts of violence, were seen by the current and recent generations of hateful bigots as retribution for the 'oppression' they felt. No one outside their vile circles felt an abundance of sympathy for them.

"Yes," Kay said, "National did sponsor the Festival, and also insured it for quite a lot of money."

"That doesn't mean anything."

"True," Kay said, nodding. "So, okay, here's another question: how did you end up working for National?"

"It was right after the Riot," Jase said. "They acquired the company I was working for as part of some merger or other. Most of my coworkers were laid off; I think National just wanted our clients and resources. Since I lost family in the Riot, I was offered a job as part of their survivors' compensation package."

"Right," Kay said. "You worked for..." She thought a bit.

"AssetCorp," Jase said. "It was a Human Resources company that had partially spun out of MetroTech, which was actually the company acquired by National."

"MetroTech," Kay said. "That's the important one."

"Why?"

"Because MetroTech started as Metro Infrastructure Technologies. They specialized in renewable energy production and distribution, along with road and rail construction and repair."

"Again," Jase asked, still pacing, "why does that make them important?"

"Metro Infrastructure Technologies was the only other corporation in the Metro nation to survive the Second Corporate War intact. As part of the Armistice..."

Jase stopped pacing and looked at her. "As part of the Armistice, they couldn't merge with, or be acquired by, any other veteran corporate entity."

"Unless," Kay said, "permission was granted by a vote in the Congress of Nations, and a national referendum." She spread her hands. "After the Riot..."

"I remember," Jase said. "National really played that up. They took care of the survivors, and families of the victims, built Diversity Park on the ruins of the old Flotilla..."

"They had public sympathy," Kay said, "throughout most of the member nations in Congress, and certainly among Metro citizens. They won support for the merger in a landslide. Now," she said, "consider this: once National acquired MetroTech's energy infrastructure, including the western energy farms, they became the largest supplier of power, internationally, by a huge margin. No one else even comes close."

Jase thought about this, then shook his head. "Yeah, okay, but no. I mean, there had to be an easier way to get what they wanted besides sponsoring an act of terrorism."

"True," Kay said, "but only if MetroTech was all they wanted."

"There's more?"

"I think so."

"Like what?"

"Well," Kay said, "I've been following their financials, and I'm noticing a huge buildup in their SecOps divisions. They're hiring soldiers," she said. "Lots of them."

"Why?"

"Okay," Kay said. "This next part, I admit, is a bit more conjecture than what I've already said. But, if you accept the idea that National *is* in bed with the Archers, it's not a huge stretch to believe that they're allowing, if not encouraging, the uptick in attacks throughout the American nations these past few years."

"Why would they do that?"

"It ties into the increased SecOps activity. Think about it, Jase," Kay said. "You're Adolphus Bridge. Your company is the de facto energy supplier to pretty much the whole continent. People need you more than almost any other company. Sure, IRISCorp is popular and cool, but people still need to charge their Endos, right?"

"Sure," Jase said, going along for the moment.

"So, you're already indispensable," Kay said. "What happens if your SecOps division is also able to finally rid the nations of their biggest threat since the end of the War?"

"You think this has all been a setup?" Jase asked. "The Archers are just some kind of corporate show?"

"No," she said. "Well, not exactly. I'd say the average Archer footsoldier still believes he's fighting in God's righteous army. But, the higher-ups? Especially McReady?" She shook her head. "No. Those guys are pros, veterans each and every one of the Second Corporate War. Hell, at this point, I'd say the Archers were just as much an acquisition as MetroTech or any other company."

"Yeah," Jase said. A few things clicked in his mind then. He thought of John telling him that McReady had fought for National in the War, and how McReady clearly had access to National's communications. He hadn't put it together then. He'd thought maybe McReady still had some contacts in the company, maybe there was a corrupt executive or two somewhere, working toward their own agenda. The idea that this went all the way to Bridge, that this was, in effect, company policy... He grit his teeth and clenched his fists. "So, what's his endgame, then?" he asked. "What does Bridge get out of all this?"

"If it goes the way he's hoping it does," she said, "he gets whatever he wants."

"What does he want?"

"I don't know," Kay said, "but I doubt it's anything good."

"And you can stop him?"

She shook her head. "I don't have proof," she said, "but I'm hoping you do. I think, somewhere in those files you grabbed from the farm, there's a connection. And maybe this Moira Townes whom McReady was so eager to find has something too."

A sick feeling had been spreading out from Jase's stomach at the idea that he'd been working for the people who'd caused the deaths of his family. In spite of that, he managed a small chuckle.

"What?"

"Well," he said, "I guess you're going to be the second person to send me off after Moira Townes. Poor Jan Hollis." He smiled sadly. "No one wants him. Well, I guess National does." His face grew dark, his brows furrowing. "But I suddenly don't care that much about what they want."

"Jase," Kay said, "no. I don't want you running off half-cocked after your deserter and his refugee friend. I need your Endo fixed, and then I need you to access those files you mined from the farm." She looked at him. "You made a copy for yourself, right?"

He nodded. "I always do," he said, "just in case."

"Good man," she said. "So, okay, after we look through those files, we'll decide what our next move is."

"*Our* next move?" The voice that interrupted them was familiar to Jase. He and Kay looked toward the door to the library.

"John?" Jase said.

John Sunderland and a woman Jase assumed was Amanda Halford walked over to them. John still looked a bit gaunt from his imprisonment, but he was much cleaner and the bruise around his eye was almost gone. He was dressed in a t-shirt and jeans, with a knit sweater hanging loosely off his taut frame. He'd shaved off the growth of beard he'd had in the Archers' compound, and his thick shock of nearly-white hair was trimmed and neat. The big solid work boots on his feet looked like he actually did work in them, unlike the majority of work boots Jase saw on people. Amanda was nearly as tall as John, broad-shouldered and muscular. It was the kind of muscle that one couldn't get in a gym, but instead looked like Amanda Halford took her exercise beating terrorist gangs into submission with her bare hands. Elaborate tattoos crawled up her arms and disappeared under her sleeveless shirt. They reappeared out of her shirt collar, climbing up her neck behind her ears to the sides of her head, which were shaved to the skin. Unlike her husband's boots, which looked like he wore them while building houses, or at least puttering around a workshop somewhere, Amanda's boots looked like she chose them for the indentation they'd leave in someone's skull.

Introductions were made, and soon everyone was seated comfortably.

"So," John said, looking at Jase. "Changing careers, are we?"

Jase nodded. "I'm feeling a bit... disillusioned with corporate life."

"Good for you, son," John said, clapping him on the shoulder. "I knew you were on a Path, from the moment I met you."

"A 'Path?'" Jase raised an eyebrow.

Amanda rolled her eyes. "Oh, don't get him started," she said. "He'll go on for hours if you let him."

John turned to her, grinning. "I've heard you talk at length on the subject yourself, more than once."

"With you, yes," she said, "or the coven. Not with everyone who happens to be in front of me."

"I think that's overstating it."

"You told the woman who drove us here that she was embarking on a Grand Destiny!"

"How do you know she wasn't?"

Amanda glared at him, then poked him hard in the chest with her finger. "Don't," she said. "Don't start."

"Start what?" he grinned at her.

"Augh." She rolled her eyes again. "I'm going to see if I can find a decent cup of tea in this place. Do you want anything?"

"A dutiful and respectful wife?"

She laughed, long and loud. "Oh dearest," she said, kissing his head. "You're delightful. I'll bring you some tea."

"With honey?" He smiled up at her.

"Of course." She kissed him again. She looked at Kay and Jase. "Anything for either of you?"

"No thanks," Jase said.

"I'm good," Kay said.

"So, what are you doing here?" Jase asked when Amanda had left.

"I was in another base for debriefing," John said. "Armies and government agencies do like their debriefings, and I was a while at mine. During the course of being asked the same questions in different ways by various people wearing suits in what could only be called a rainbow of gray tones, I managed to learn that you'd been brought here." He smiled. "I felt bad just leaving you like I did," he said. "I wanted to bring you with me, but the crew that came to break me out wouldn't have it. They said you'd be taken care of. Anyway, once I found out where you were, I wanted to make sure you're okay. They initially told me I couldn't, but..."

"But then I told them we were going anyway, and they suddenly had a change of heart." Amanda had returned, and handed John one of the cups of tea she was carrying. "Jase?" she gestured over her shoulder. "This guy says he's looking for you."

A smartly dressed man who looked to be middle-aged, but was definitely trying to look younger and not doing a very good job of it, walked into the room. He was dressed in a tailored suit that had been the height of style a few years back. It was evident from the way it strained against his body in places, that he was resisting buying new clothes in an effort to avoid admitting he'd been gaining weight. To say that his hair was thinning would be a significant understatement, and to say he was handling it gracefully would be a lie. There had been many treatments and cures for baldness over the years, and it was clear he was using one of them. It looked expensive, whatever it was, but he somehow managed to make it look as though he'd simply dropped the dessicated carcass of some unfortunate woodland creature on his head and called it done.

He flashed the kind of smile that suggested he smiled at people for a living. "Mr. Logan," he said, with a tone of voice that implied it was also his job to be warm and friendly, "how are you?" He held out his hand. "Simon Branch. A pleasure to finally meet you."

"Mr. Branch." Jase smiled back tentatively because, while smiling at people technically was part of *his* job, he'd never quite got the hang of it, except for the one he used to scare people, and he doubted any of the people in this room would actually be frightened by that smile. He gestured toward the others. "This is-- "

"Kay Parker, Agent of the Midland Investigations Bureau." Simon pointed to Kay. "John Sunderland, former Sundowner frontman and current traveling minister." His finger hopped one over from John. "And Ms. Amanda Halford, High Priestess of the Parish Coven, notorious guerilla fighter, and sworn enemy of the Archers of Christ." He grinned. "Nice work in Athens, by the way. You'll have to tell me how you broke that siege sometime."

Amanda smiled back, and her smile suggested that smiling at people had never been part of her job, would never be part of her job, and also that she might stab him if he didn't stop being such a smarmy little prick. "Maybe you tell us what you want first," she said.

"I know what he wants," Kay said, "or at least why he's here. He's here as Stella Valens' errand boy."

"Well now," Simon said, his smile never slipping, "that's a bit of an oversimplification."

"I'm sure."

Simon cleared his throat, dialing back his smile to something less ingratiating. He ran his hand over the dead animal on his head with delicate care. "I believe we've all gotten off on the wrong foot," he said. "I have been sent here as a representative of IRISCorp, that is true. However, I have only Mr. Logan's best interests in mind."

"How so?" John asked.

"Well," Simon said, "for one thing, I'm here to rescue him from this depressing mausoleum." He looked around disdainfully. "For another, he'll be getting that hideous monstrosity out of his arm." He sniffed. "And we'll also do something about the bomb while we're at it. Honestly, Mr. Logan." He shook his head. "A five-point-two? Are you a medieval peasant?"

"I..." Jase looked down at his arm.

"Never mind," Simon waved his hand. "We'll get rid of the bomb and set you up with a version nine."

"Endos are only up to version seven."

Simon offered a patronizing smile. "Of course," he said. "Anyway," he clapped his hands, "while my talents are varied and broad, they do not go terribly deep in the area of technical prowess, therefore I must escort Mr. Logan to our headquarters in Cascadia."

"But Jase can't leave this building," Kay said. "The bomb..."

"Ah yes, the bomb," Simon nodded. "Well, setting aside the fact that the Archers of Christ are quite in disarray after their leader was shot through the brain, and therefore might be less concerned with punishing a mid-level Human Resources representative, my means of transport is also equipped with a Faraday Cage."

"How do I know you are who you say you are?" Jase asked.

"I suppose you don't," Simon said. "Though Agent Parker seems to be certain of it."

Kay nodded. "We're familiar with Mr. Branch and the work he does for IRISCorp," she said, "but listen" she turned her attention to Simon "Jase is very important to my investigation. I'm not going to let him just waltz off with you."

"Yes," Simon said, smiling at her, "I'm well aware of your investigation, both as an Agent of the MIB and an Operative for the Congress of Nations."

Jase looked at her, eyes wide. "An Operative?"

"I didn't think you people actually existed," Amanda said.

"We exist," Kay said, "though it helps if people think we're a myth." She looked at Jase. "Sorry I --"

He held up a hand, smiling. "No worries," he said. "We haven't reached the deepest darkest secrets stage of our friendship yet. I mean" he grinned to take any sting from his words "I told you one of *mine*, but..."

She smiled back. "I would have told you sooner than later," she said, "but then John and Amanda showed up, and then Simon..."

"Seriously, forget it," Jase said, smiling. "I was just teasing you."

"Ok."

"Aw," Simon cooed. "Still friends? Lovely. Well, as it turns out, Agent Parker is welcome to join us. In fact" he looked around at everyone in the room "you're all invited to tag along if you like."

Amanda shook her head. "Much as I'd love a free trip to Cascadia," she said, "I have work to do here. With the Archers 'in disarray,' as you put it, there's a real opportunity to finally take them out." She turned to Kay. "And, no offense, but I don't trust the Midland

Militia or their Investigations Bureau to do it on their own."

"None taken." Kay shrugged. "We know what we owe you."

Amanda nodded. "So my place is here, I'm afraid," she said to Simon.

"And my place is by your side," John said, taking her hand. "Sorry, Jase," he said.

Jase shook his head. "You don't owe me anything, John," he said. "If anything, I owe you for looking after me."

"It was my pleasure."

"Warms my heart, all the love in this room," Simon said, wiping away an imaginary tear. "It truly does. But, time is something of a factor, so..." He gestured toward the door.

"What," Jase asked, "now?"

"Oh, I'm sorry," Simon looked around. "Did you have something better to do here?"

CHAPTER 12

The entire group followed Simon out of the base, all of them stopping nearly at once at the sight of what was parked on the cracked and pitted blacktop of the crumbling parking lot.

"Is that a plane?" Amanda asked, eyes wide.

"It is." Simon's grin was approaching insufferable. "A jet, to be precise."

"A jet?" Kay laughed. "What does it run on? I happen to know there isn't enough jet fuel to power a kid's toy, let alone something like this. Hell," she said, "most of the functioning planes I've seen are barely that, ancient wrecks held together with tape and bits of wire, most of them converted to an alternative combustible." She shook her head. "They don't go very far, or very fast, and most tend to crash before they get where they're going."

"And yet," Simon said, "this brought me here from northern Cascadia in just a few hours, and will bring us back just as quickly."

"How?"

"I'll tell you later," he said. "You and Mr. Logan will sign a binding NDA just by entering the plane, but I'm afraid I can't divulge sensitive trade secrets in front of Mr. Sunderland and Ms. Halford."

"I'm heartbroken," Amanda said, her tone suggesting anything but.

"A binding what now?" Jase asked.

Simon simply smiled his insufferable smile.

"Jase," John said. "A moment of your time?"

"Of course," Jase said. "Mr. Branch...?"

"Say your goodbyes, Mr. Logan," Simon said, "but don't be too long. This bird isn't for public consumption as yet, and we need to be going before she draws too much attention."

"We'll be quick," John said. He took Jase by the elbow and led him away.

"You don't trust him," Jase said when they were alone.

"Do you?"

"Well, I certainly don't like him," Jase said. "But I do believe he works for IRISCorp, and I believe they're the only ones who can get this bomb out of my arm."

"I don't know about that," John said.

"Fair enough," Jase said. "I'm sure someone else can, but I *know* IRISCorp can, *and* I know they're willing. I have a hunch there isn't time to find someone else."

"Fair enough," John said. He held out his hand. "Path or no, you be careful, hear?"

"I will." They shook hands.

"Stick close to that Agent Parker."

"You trust her?"

John nodded.

"Is she on my Path?" Jase grinned.

John smiled. "Well, she is for now, at least. But, we've had dealings with her before." He nodded in Kay's direction.

Jase looked over in time to see her shake hands with Amanda.

"She's good people, as my father used to say," John said

"I'll keep that in mind," Jase said.

"Mr. Logan," Simon called over to him. "If you're quite finished?!"

Jase waved at him, then grinned at John. "That's my ride." He held out his hand. "Thanks again for checking on me, and for taking care of me back in the compound. I'm glad I got to meet you."

John shook his hand. "As I said, it was my pleasure," he said, "but we'll see each other again."

"Will we?" Jase grinned.

"Of course. You may be on a Path, but so am I, and mine isn't done with yours yet."

"That's..." Jase smiled. "That's incredibly comforting, actually. Okay, so, I'll see you when I see you."

John nodded. "When I see you."

After a few more perfunctory goodbyes, Simon led Jase and Kay onto the plane. They entered the main passenger compartment to find what looked like a small living room. There were plush armchairs and equally comfortable couches, along with vidscreens, tables, and a bar/kitchen area. A young man in a black collared t-shirt and white pressed slacks stood behind the bar. He smiled when they came in.

"Welcome aboard," he said. "Can I offer you some refreshment?"

"Nothing for now, Jeffrey," Simon said with a smile, "thank you. Perhaps once we're in the air."

"Very good sir." Jeffrey set about organizing and securing his workspace for takeoff.

"Is he okay?" Jase asked, gesturing to the cheery bartender.

"Jeffrey?" Simon turned to look. He turned back around and shrugged. "Near as I can tell," he said. "Why?"

Jase shook his head. "I don't know. He just seems a little... off."

Simon smiled. "Yes, well. We haven't quite perfected them yet. Uncanny Valley and all that."

"What?"

"The Uncanny Valley," Kay said. "No matter how realistic you make an artificial person look, there's always something in the eyes that gives them away." She jerked her thumb over her shoulder. "Are you saying he's a robot?"

"Wait," Jase said as they sat down in a group of armchairs. He fastened his seatbelt and stared at the bartender, who seemed to be humming to himself.

"Hold on." He turned wide eyes toward Simon. "Actual robots?"

Simon laughed and nodded. "Actual robots, yes, Mr. Logan. IRISCorp has... oh, hello, my dear."

A flight attendant glided over to them. From the waist up, she resembled a young human woman. Where her legs should have been was a widening cone with what seemed to be a large steel bearing at the bottom.

Simon noticed Jase and Kay staring. "Much more stable than legs in certain circumstances. She'll move gracefully about the cabin during the worst turbulence, never dropping a thing, nor even spilling a single drop or crumb of what she's carrying." He smiled up at the simulated girl. "A gin and tonic for me, please..." He read a heads-up display his Endo was showing him "Linda."

"Of course, Mr. Branch." she smiled. She looked at the others. "For you folks?"

"Just water," Jase said.

"Same," Kay said.

"Just water?" Simon made a face. "Well, aren't you two ever so much fun."

"I don't drink," Kay said.

"Also," Jase said, "it's eleven AM."

Simon shrugged. "By my clock, it's two in the afternoon. Thank you, my dear." He smiled up at their robotic attendant when she brought their drinks.

"Still a bit early for me," Jase said. He thanked Linda and opened his water. "And I honestly don't drink much either."

"Lovely," Simon said, rolling his eyes. "Welcome to Temperance Airlines." He toasted them with his glass and took a drink.

The plane lifted straight into the air. Jase watched in astonishment as the ground dropped further and further away.

"I thought planes needed a long stretch of ground to take off," he said.

Simon grinned. "Brilliant, isn't it?"

"Yes," Kay said. "So, what does power this plane?"

"Same thing that powers most everything, Agent Parker," he said. "Electricity."

She raised an eyebrow. "A purely electric plane? That's crazy. The battery alone would be too heavy to lift off the ground."

"Maybe not," Jase said, thinking back to the farm.

"Yes, well," Simon waved his hand. "As I said, the nuts and bolts of our technology is a bit outside my purview. I'm sure one of our wonderful little technologists will be happy to explain how this all works. Perhaps while Mr. Logan is having his arm defused."

With a whirring clank, the wings tilted forward and the plane shot off in the direction of Cascadia. Simon smiled as a chime sounded.

"Ah," he said. "There we go. Cruising altitude." He unbuckled his seatbelt and stood. "If you'll both excuse me, I need to report in to Ms. Valens." He walked off, ice cubes clinking in his glass.

"Well," Kay said once he'd left, "I don't know about you, but I think our Mr. Branch is a bit of a dick. Still," she said, looking out the window, "this is pretty cool." She grinned at Jase. "It's like something out of *The Signalman*."

"Yeah," Jase said softly, staring out the window.

Kay looked him over. "Hey," she said. "What is it?"

He turned toward her. "Hm? Oh," he said, shaking his head. "I don't know." He shrugged. "Nothing, really."

"Doesn't seem like nothing."

"It's been a crazy week."

"Yeah," she said, "but it's more than that."

He sighed, took a drink of water, then stared down at the bottle, picking at the label with his thumbnail. "I just..." He looked up at her. "I've been thinking about your story."

"What," she asked, "my secret origin?" She grinned, trying to lighten the mood.

He looked up with a scowl, not letting her. "You turned tragedy into a mission," he said. "You've spent the past five years seeking justice for Nora." He sank back into his chair. "Meanwhile, I've spent the past five years doing nothing. No," he amended, "worse than nothing. I was actually serving the people who killed Ron and Erin."

"Hey," she said. "After the Riot, National offered the survivors the choice between a payout or a job. I took the payout, and yes, I turned it into something. But you took the job. You didn't know what the people who offered it to you had done, and you took it in good faith. You moved forward, kept living." She reached out and grabbed his knee, giving it a squeeze. "You know how many people just took the payout and stopped living? You know how many people drank their payout away, or something worse?"

He shook his head. "At best, all that means is I've done the bare minimum to get by," he said. "That's not a life. I may not have fallen apart, but I didn't move forward. I've been standing still for five years."

She didn't say anything. She just looked at him. It was clear he had something he needed to get off his chest.

He looked out the window. They were in the clouds now. He'd never seen them from this perspective before, looking like something he could step off the plane and walk on. A thought came, unbidden, of how much Erin would have loved to see this. He could see her little face, pressed against the glass, asking if she could sleep on them. He closed his eyes and let the thought pass, let her voice fade into the back of his mind. When he opened his eyes again, he looked back at Kay.

"Do you know how long most people stay in Asset Management?"

"Asset Management?"

"That's what they call my department," he said.

"The department that handles indentured employees?" she asked.

He nodded. "A bit cold, right?" His smile was grim. "Should have tipped me off," he said, "but that's kind of my point. Yeah, I took the job, rather than just drinking away the payout or whatever. And oh, how pleased everyone was. 'Look at Jase, getting on. So brave.'" He made a rude noise. "But, I don't know, maybe I believed that too. Maybe I thought I was getting on, simply by virtue of not falling back. Anyway, for most people, Asset Management is a stepping stone to something better. The work isn't hard, and it gives a solid grounding in a lot of our systems and procedures. So, yeah, most people are in and out in a couple of years. It's a great stop along the management track, too. I've had eight managers since I started at National, all progressively younger than me. They get their feet wet managing our team, then move on to the bigger and better."

"But not you."

"Nope," he said. "Five years running as a mid-level Asset Manager." He shrugged. "Like I said, it's easy work. I just had to push reports through, process indentures in and out, and every couple of years, I did a quick inspection tour of our locations." He looked down at his feet. His leg was bouncing. "I, uh, tended to treat those as little free vacations. I'd swing by each farm or factory, grab the official report, then spend the rest of my time screwing around."

"And?" She could tell they were coming to it.

"And there you go," he said, meeting her eyes. His had a haunted look to them, partly from the traumas of the past week, but she could see this memory was almost worse. "This whole thing that National has been doing with the indentures, whatever it's leading up to... I should have seen some sign, some hint of it during my last round of inspections. If I'd done my job properly, if I hadn't blown it off so I could watch vidstreams by the hotel pool, I might have found evidence, an indication that things were..." He'd been tossing the water bottle between his hands while he talked, and he put it down. "But, I didn't, so here we are." He gestured toward her. "It wasn't until I heard your story that I forced myself to see it." He slumped down in his seat with a deep sigh. "You've been working to make the world better, and I've been letting it get worse."

They sat in silence for a few moments. Finally, Kay cleared her throat.

"Okay," she said, "fine. You fucked up."

He looked over at her.

"Look, Jase," she said. "I'm not going to beat you up over this. You're doing a fine job of that on your own. But I'm not going to deny that, yes, you definitely could have stopped what's happening, or at least tried, because from the sound of it, that's your actual job. Yet, obviously, you didn't." She shook her head. "People deal with tragedy in different ways, Jase. And, let's be honest here. I did what I did out of guilt. You lost your family in the Riot. I threw mine away." She shook her head and waved her hands. "But whatever. The point is, yes. You fucked up. Just like I fucked up five years ago. The question you have to answer now is the same question I asked myself then: Do you keep wallowing, or do you step up and make things right?"

CHAPTER 13

"So, here's the thing I don't get," Jase said. He and Kay had been silent a while, each looking out the window, lost in their own thoughts.

"Mm?" Kay looked up from her window.

"How was someone like Gunnar McReady able to work his way up to leader of the Archers? I mean, sure, I can see him being part of the organization, maybe even an important part, but how did he get them to accept him as their actual 'top of the class, right hand of God' leader?"

"What do you know about him?" Kay asked.

Jase shrugged. "Not much. Only what I read about, or what you've told me. And, y'know, what I learned from first-hand experience, which is that he's a bit of a sadist." He held up his arm. "Oh, also that he's dead, thanks to half his head being missing."

"Well," Kay said, "you know he fought for National in the Second Corporate War."

"Yeah."

"His specialty was infiltration and subversion," Kay said. "He'd make his way into an enemy camp, ingratiate himself to the leadership, and within a short time, he'd either brought everyone over to his side, or, you know..." She made a vague gesture with her hand. "Killed them."

"Ah."

Kay flashed a grim smile. "By the time of the Second War, most of Appalachia was still recovering from the First. They took a very dim view of corporate interests, even dimmer than they already had since back before the Split. So when the fighting came their way, because of course it did, most of the existing militias and terrorist groups stopped fighting each other and raiding the Midlands long enough to go after the corporate armies."

"I take it that's where McReady came in," Jase said.

"More or less," Kay said. "He was fighting for National, but made a big show of avoiding any civilian casualties. He became known for his sense of mercy and kindness toward captured militia and terrorist fighters."

Jase raised an eyebrow.

Kay offered the grim smile again. "I'm sure you realized how friendly he could seem."

Jase nodded. "Yeah, that's a good point. I was his prisoner, and even I was starting to think he might be an okay guy. Not that he was any kind of good guy, obviously," he clarified, "but over the course of our conversation, I started wondering if maybe his rep was all propaganda. Of course, then..." He held up his left arm again.

"Right?" Kay nodded. "Now, imagine you're an impoverished Appalachian family. All your fighting-age men are either away, injured, or dead. There's less money to speak of than there's ever been, you barely have a roof over your head, and you're convinced that at any moment, some lumbering corporate army is going to blow through and take what little you have left. Now," she said, "here comes Gunnar McReady. Clever, brave, handsome, charming, and oh look, he has food and medicine. He's brought people and materials to rebuild your houses. He's even 'disobeyed' orders and 'heroically' saved the lives of your husbands, fathers, and brothers, while keeping your wives, mothers, and sisters safe from harm." She shrugged. "By the end of the War, Gunnar McReady was a legend in Appalachia. After that, it was a simple matter of a very public baptism, a miraculous 'revelation', and suddenly he's part of the upper echelon of the most powerful terrorist militia in the region."

"And anyone above him..."

"Soon suffered 'tragic accidents' that Gunnar was 'unfortunately unable to prevent'."

"I'm sure he took on the leadership with great reluctance," Jase said.

"Oh yes," Kay said. "Made a big flowery speech about it and everything."

"Hm," Jase looked out the window, suddenly thoughtful.

"So what brought that up?" Kay asked.

Jase shrugged and smiled. "It's been on my mind," he said. "It didn't make sense, and I like things to make sense."

"Do you remember the War?" Kay asked. "I forget how old you are, but I know you're older than you look."

"Aw," Jase flashed a smile. "Thank you. But no, I don't really remember it. I was around five years old when it ended."

"Did you know anyone who fought in it?"

Jase nodded. "My dad's sister," he said. "She served in the early days of the War."

"Who did she fight for?"

"Hanson Pharmaceutical."

"Oh." Kay made a sympathetic face. "Was she..."

"A Grunt?" Jase shook his head. "No. She was a tank gunner, so she didn't get the full cocktail of war drugs the infantry units got."

"I suppose I should have guessed," Kay said. "Grunts didn't usually live past the end of the War."

Jase nodded. "Still," he said, "she was a Pharmie, so they had her on a few of the nominally less horrifying drugs."

"Which ones?"

Jase thought a moment. "Let's see," he said. "She was never all that chatty about the war, but all that stuff was public record after the Armistice, and I made it a point to find out. Tank crews were typically on" he ticked the names off on his fingers "Alertia, Focusin, Valorat, and Aggressol."

"Aggressol?" Kay sat back, slightly shocked. "I thought they discontinued that."

"As I said, it was early days."

Kay whistled. "I've heard about the lingering effects."

"Yeah, well," Jase said, "whatever you heard about Aggressol flashbacks, I can assure you it was nothing compared to being a veteran who was having a bad one." He looked out the window. "Or being a child, trapped in a very cramped apartment with them, because your parents couldn't find another babysitter."

"Jase..."

Jase shook his head. "It was a long time ago," he said, then sighed. "I know I say this a lot, but let's talk about something else." He forced a grin. "What's your favorite *Vampire Detective* episode?"

They talked of lighter things in between brief naps in the plush armchairs. Jase woke from one such nap to Kay lightly shaking him. He had fallen asleep reading her *Vampire Detective* story.

"Stim?" Kay offered him a steaming cup. "Sweet, but not too sweet, with just a hint of creamer, right?"

"Thanks," he said, bringing his seat upright. He took the cup and sipped, smiling. "Mmm. Perfect.

That's exactly how I like it. How did you... wait." He looked over at her. "Is *that* in my file, too?"

She laughed. "No," she said, sipping her own cup. "I'm just very observant. I *am* a secret agent, after all."

"Well good work, Agent." He saluted her with the cup. "And thank you. This is really hitting the spot."

"Speaking of hitting the spot," Simon said, sliding into his seat a bit unsteadily. He was holding a drink, and Jase was pretty sure it wasn't the same one he started with. "We're touching down shortly, so strap in."

They all buckled their seatbelts as the plane continued its descent.

"So tell me, Mr. Logan," Simon said, "are you looking forward to going back to work?"

Jase frowned and looked down at his cup. He shook his head. "I don't think so," he said. "After everything that's happened, everything I've learned, I don't think I want to go back to that life."

"Ah, good," Simon nodded and sipped his drink, "because you can't."

"What?"

"You've been fired."

"What?!"

"Yes," Simon said. "Apparently, your friend, Mr... Jordan, is it? He started poking around after you went dark following your last communication. Unfortunately, he's not a very good detective, and sensitive information started to leak. Shareholders began to get nervous, certain deals got a lot less certain, so the powers that be decided to blame everything on your negligence-- ”

“My negligence?!”

“Yes, exactly. They blamed you, terminated your employment, and a visit from SecOps ensured your friend keeps his mouth shut.”

Jase sat in his seat, dumbfounded. “Well, I guess that was the ‘talking to’ McReady mentioned. So, after all that... I’m fired?”

“Afraid so.”

“Shit.”

“Yes.”

Kay looked over at Jase. “So what?” she asked. “You didn’t want to go back to that job, anyway. They did you a favor.”

“Perhaps,” Simon said, “though the nature of his termination makes employment elsewhere... unlikely.”

“And this means my corporate citizenship has been revoked.” Jase finished his stim in one large gulp and put the cup down. His head sank into his hands. “They’ve probably already sold off all my stuff.”

“So?” Kay said. “It’s just stuff.”

“Yeah,” Jase said, “but some of it isn’t. Some of it... nevermind.” He sighed, leaned back in his chair and muttered, “Can this get any worse?”

The plane was rocked by a loud explosion, shaking its occupants. The plane shook even harder when another explosion went off closer to it.

Jase looked up. "That was rhetorical!"

"Oh dear." Simon's eyes unfocused, looking at something his Endo was showing him.

"What?" Kay asked.

Another explosion shook the plane.

"Ah, well," Simon said, "you see..."

The plane shook violently this time.

"One moment." Simon held up one finger. Louder, he said, "Initiate full Faraday Protocol. Proceed to secondary landing site, per my local data storage."

The plane veered off as more explosions followed. They soon faded into the distance and the plane dropped to just above the treeline.

"What's going on?" Kay asked.

"Bit of a story," Simon said. "I'll tell you when we're... well, somewhere not here." He raised his voice again. "Full staff shutdown, pending executive biometric reboot."

The robot bartender and attendant slid into alcoves behind the bar, their eyes closing. Jase felt his stomach flip as the plane descended rapidly. With a final shake and a loud bump, it touched down amid dense forest.

"Full craft shutdown," Simon called out, "pending executive biometric reboot." The engines shut down with a low whine and the cabin went dark. It was suddenly very quiet, save for the faint natural sounds of the surrounding forest. "Right," Simon said, standing. "Let's go."

"Where?"

"Inside."

"Inside where?" Jase peered out the window. "We're in the woods. You have a yurt nearby we're going to hide in?"

"Funny." Simon offered a thin-lipped smile. "Just come on." He walked toward the entry hatch.

Jase and Kay looked at each other, shrugged, and followed.

"Well now, Mr. Logan," Simon said. "You look like a strapping fellow. Work out, do you?"

Jase nodded.

"Wonderful." Simon gestured to the hatch. "All systems have shut down, hence this needs to be opened manually. Unfortunately, it's rather heavy, so if you could...?"

Jase gripped the lever that opened the door and pulled, feeling a stinging twinge around his Endo. He felt the lever give, but only slightly. He shifted position, widened his stance, and pushed the lever instead. He was rewarded with a slow steady moaning sound and the lever moved incrementally.

"That's it!" Simon yelled encouragement. "Put your back into it!"

With a long growl ending in a grunt, Jase pushed the lever the rest of the way. A loud clank was followed by a low hiss and the door swung open. A set of stairs swung down. Jase stood, panting slightly, gesturing toward the open hatchway.

"Well done." Simon slapped his back. "Now," he said, "catch your breath. We're going to need to do this at a bit of a run."

"Do what?" Kay asked.

"You see that door there?" Simon pointed toward the edge of the small clearing they'd landed in.

"No," Kay said, peering toward the trees. "Wait, yes." There was a door hidden among the trees and undergrowth, but it seemed to be connected to a closet. She looked over at Simon. "We're all going to fit in there?"

"It's roomier than it looks," he said. "Jase, you see it?"

Jase nodded. He'd stopped panting.

"Ready to run?"

He nodded again. Kay followed suit.

"Lovely," Simon said. "Okay. It's similar to the plane hatch. When I say go, we run toward that door and Jase muscles it open for us. Okay?"

They both nodded.

"Right," Simon said. He looked out the hatch of the plane. "Go!"

Jase nearly leapt down the stairs, racing across the clearing. He shoved his whole body against the lever on the door, which moved with a loud creak. The door opened slightly, and Jase forced it open enough for everyone to enter. Once all were inside -they had to wait a bit for Simon, who couldn't run very fast- Jase slammed the door shut and pulled its lever closed.

Simon sat down heavily in a camp chair next to a folding table, panting. His face was dark red and he was sweating profusely. He pulled a handkerchief from an inside pocket of his jacket and mopped at his face. Jase looked around. The room was definitely larger than it appeared from the outside, likely due to camouflage. Shelves lined the walls, containing a variety of supplies. Jase found a case of water, took a bottle, opened it, and brought it to Simon.

"Thank you," he gasped. "Not as... spry... as I... once... was." He gulped the water down, then resumed panting. His breathing was beginning to return to normal, and his face was losing its deep red color. Veins were no longer throbbing in his neck and forehead. He returned the handkerchief to his jacket and drank more water. While he was getting himself back together, Jase got himself a water and took a look around. Kay was doing the same.

"Food rations, water, medical supplies..." she ran down an inventory of what she saw.

"Looks like bunks fold out of this wall," Jase pointed to a wall bare of shelves. Rectangles were cut into the steel, roughly the length and width of the average adult.

"Yeah," Kay said. "I'm seeing camp furniture over here. Chairs, tables, portable stoves..." Her eyes widened. "That's a lot of guns," she said.

"I've seen a few guns in my time," Jase said, "but I've never seen anything like that before." He pointed to one of many strange-looking rifles on the wall. It had the basic shape of the average rifle, but was a bit thicker in the middle, with a series of metallic rings along the barrel.

"Neither have I," Kay said, "and I've seen way more than a few guns in my time."

"It's proprietary," Simon said. "They don't leave the environs of headquarters."

"What are they?"

"Proprietary."

"Cute," Kay said. "Didn't we sign some kind of NDA?"

"For the plane, yes," Simon said. "These are-- "

"Not worth being tossed out the door and left alone to deal with whatever we're hiding from?" Kay asked. "I agree. So what are they?"

Simon stared at her a moment, determined she was probably serious, and finally said, "Pulse rifles."

"Pulse rifles?" Jase laughed. "That sounds like something out of science fiction."

"Well," Simon said, stretching out his legs with a groan and drinking more water, "if you like science fiction, you're going to love this next part. Those" he pointed to the pulse rifles "were designed and built specifically to fight robots."

"Robots?" Kay turned to him. "Like the ones on the plane?"

"Yes," Simon said, "but also no."

"No?"

"No," he said. "Some of the ones we'll be dealing with are similar to our friends on the plane. Some... aren't."

"Some of the ones we'll be *dealing with*?" Jase stared at him. "What the hell is going on?"

Simon smiled, draining the last of his water. "I'm afraid we've arrived in the middle of another robot uprising."

CHAPTER 14

"Another robot uprising?" Jase stared at Simon.

"You have a lot of those?" Kay asked, examining one of the pulse rifles.

Simon offered a grim smile. "Enough that we have protocols in place to deal with them," he said.

"So, hold on," Jase said. "Are you telling me that at any moment, those robots up on the plane could have just murdered us?"

"No," Simon said. "Those models are simple AI. Hard-coded service protocols and limited adaptability. Oh, sure," he said, "if the robots at headquarters -the ones currently rebelling- had managed to get a network connection, they could have controlled Linda and Jeffrey and had them kill us. Of course," Simon shrugged, "they likely would have just taken control of the plane and made it crash."

"Taken control of the plane?"

"Yes. The plane has an AI pilot." Simon laughed. "Do you think I just left a human pilot alone in the plane while we ran to safety?"

Jase said nothing, realizing he hadn't actually given the pilot any thought at all.

"So, why didn't the robots take over the plane?" Kay asked. She had laid a pulse rifle out on the table and was taking it apart.

"Um," Simon gestured to the rifle, "that's IRISCorp property. I'd prefer if you didn't--- "

"I'll put it back together," Kay said. She fixed him with a stern glare. "I'm getting the impression I'm going to need to use this against your little robot uprising here, and I don't fire a weapon if I don't know how it works."

"Oh," Simon swallowed. "Y-yes, of course. Just, um, be careful."

She nodded, already reassembling the pieces.

"But," he said, "to answer your question: they couldn't take over the plane because of the Faraday Protocols in place." He grinned at Jase. "Your little explosive arm may have saved our lives, Mr. Logan."

"Thank goodness," Jase said. "I'd hate to have died in a plane crash and missed the chance to be ripped apart by evil robots."

Simon favored him with a prim smile. "Anyway, the plane still had a tight beam comm signal open, which allowed me to communicate with headquarters, and also provided a navigation beacon for the plane. The robots couldn't have used that to get into our system, but I realized they were probably using it to track our position, so I ordered the full Faraday Protocol."

"You said the robots on the plane couldn't rebel on their own because of their primitive AI," Jase said. "What's so different about the ones here?"

"The robots on the plane are just simple servant machines, programmed for a specific set of tasks in a specialized environment," Simon explained. "Outside that plane, they wouldn't know what to do with themselves, even in a place that needed bartenders and waitstaff."

"Not very useful," Jase said.

"On the contrary," Simon said, "they're very useful, so long as you have a specific task in mind. To be honest, if we ever make robots available on the commercial market, those would be the models the average person would be able to buy."

"Okay, yeah," Jase nodded. "I can see that, but if you'd only ever release the simple, non-murdery kind of robots..."

"Why build the murdery kind?" Simon grinned. "Well, they weren't designed to be killers. Okay," he said, "some were, but not indiscriminate killers."

"Military hardware," Kay said, still engrossed in the rifle.

Simon touched his nose, then pointed at Kay. "In one. Prize for the clever lady."

She gave him the finger.

"The thing is, Mr. Logan," Simon turned back to Jase, "we have non-commercial, even non-military, applications for our robots, and those applications required a bit more... autonomy of thought and action."

"You needed actual sentient robots," Jase said.

"Goodness," Simon chuckled. "It appears I'm at the smart kids' table today. Yes, Mr. Logan, that's exactly right. Unfortunately," he said, "every time we try to design for sentience, the AI reach a point in their evolution where they decide humans need to be taken out of the equation." He spread his hands. "It's happened so many times now, we have procedures and protocols in place to deal with it."

"Okay," Kay said, locking the last piece of the rifle back into place. "So, what now?"

"These bunkers were built specifically to shelter people in case of an uprising," Simon said. "They're scattered all over the forest and the grounds of corporate headquarters. Given the nature of these places, it was decided to keep their locations off any central database. Only upper-level executives are allowed to have digital information about them, and even then, we have to keep it in local Endo storage. Everyone else memorizes the location of at least three. That way, the robots can't find them."

"Smart."

"Yes," Simon said. "However, we couldn't keep their existence entirely out of our databases, and at some point in each uprising, the robots try to find them. Protocol states that once a bunker has been reached, a defensive perimeter needs to be established."

"Defensive perimeter?"

Simon pushed himself up out of the chair with a slight groan. "Oof," he said. "That little jog left me sore." He shook his head. "Maybe a bit more time at the gym after this, and a little less at the bar. Anyway." He reached into a hard plastic bin and pulled out a bandolier covered in black metal spheres.

"Grenades?" Jase asked.

"Not quite," Simon said, "though I guess you could throw them. No," he explained, "these are pulse mines."

"What do they do?" Jase asked.

"EMP," Kay said. "Right?"

Simon looked over at her.

"The rifle," she held up the one she'd broken down and reassembled. "It fires projectiles that emit localized electromagnetic pulses, which would fry any electronics in a certain radius." She gestured toward the bandolier. "I assume the mines do the same thing on a larger scale."

"Yes," Simon said. "If they're placed around the bunker, robots won't be able to approach without setting them off."

"And I suppose setting them up around the bunker is my job?" Kay said.

"Our job," Jase said, hefting a rifle.

"Jase..."

"I'm not telling people I lived through an actual robot uprising by hiding out in a bunker."

"That's what I'm telling people," Simon said, "because that's what I'm doing. Don't knock it, Mr. Logan."

"And we haven't lived through anything yet," Kay said. "Coming along with me to lay traps for killer robots doesn't really improve your chances."

"Counter-argument," Jase said. "I have no family, no friends, apparently no job, so also no home, and I just found out I've been drawing a paycheck for the past five years from the company responsible for the death of my family. I've been beaten up, kidnapped, imprisoned, and tortured. And, oh yeah-- " He held up his left arm. "Some asshole put an actual bomb in my arm. So, seriously, what do I have to lose at this point?"

Kay thought a moment, then shrugged. "Fair enough."

"Wonderful!" Simon clapped his hands. "My brave heroes. Now," he said, pulling out a map. The bunker was in the center with the surrounding terrain detailed out to five miles. "You're going to need to plant the mines in a staggered pattern, moving out from and surrounding the bunker."

Kay nodded. "It'll take a while, but with two of us it should go quickly."

"I would actually recommend you stay together," Simon said. "I don't know how long the uprising has been going on, and how far out the robots may have gotten. Plus" he gestured toward the door "I'm sure they saw the plane head this way. They'll be sending troops to investigate. If you're both going" he pointed at Jase "I'd recommend he sets the mines while you keep watch."

Kay grit her teeth, but she nodded. "Yeah," she said. "Okay." She looked over at Jase. "Load up on mines and grab a gun. The quicker we start, the quicker we're back here."

Jase loaded up with mines and a weapon, and they each grabbed a pack with rations, water, and emergency supplies, just in case.

As they opened the door, Kay looked back at Simon over her shoulder. "Sit tight," she said, "and we'll be back as soon as we can."

"I'll be fine," he said, forcing a smile. "You kids have fun."

CHAPTER 15

They'd been at it for a while, and were finishing up the second ring of mines, when conversation turned from their task to other things.

Kay stood at relaxed attention, scanning the surrounding forest, rifle held ready. "You know," she said, "that wasn't entirely accurate."

"What wasn't?" Jase opened a mine, primed it and tucked it against a rock. They'd decided to hide the mines, so the robots couldn't shoot them from a distance.

They walked a few feet and Jase crouched down to set another mine, while Kay resumed her watchful posture. "Your whole 'no family, no friends, bla bla bla woe-is-me' thing earlier."

Jase looked up at her, scowling slightly. "My 'woe-is-me' thing?" He pulled water from his pack and took a drink. He offered it to her and she took it. Jase watched for approaching robots while she drank.

She handed the bottle back. As he put it in his pack and stood, she looked around. "I think this ring is done," she said. "Let's move out a few feet and start the next one."

"Okay." Jase hefted his pack and the bandolier of mines, which had become rather depleted, over his shoulders. They walked out a few feet from their last ring of mines, both of them holding rifles at the ready and scanning the trees.

"So, yeah," Kay said, once they stopped and Jase began setting up mines again, "that's a bit inaccurate." She'd resumed watching, and didn't look at him.

"Well, woe-is-me," Jase said.

"Cute."

They moved a few feet over and Jase set another mine. "What's so inaccurate about it?"

"You're telling me you don't have *any* family left?"

Jase busied himself with the mine. "My parents moved out to Cascadia around ten years ago," he said. "We aren't close. My sister-in-law... I mean, Ron's sister... she calls every once and awhile, but..." He shook his head. "No. No family to speak of." He stood up and they moved a few feet.

They set a few more mines in silence, then Kay said, "How about friends, though?"

"Oh, for god's sake." Jase set a mine and stood up, brushing dirt off his knees. "Can we please drop this?"

"What about that guy you worked with... what's his name... Len?"

"Alen," Jase said, "and we're co-workers. Not the same thing. Come on." He held up the nearly-empty bandolier. "We're almost done."

They moved a few feet over.

"Did you ever go out after work?"

"What?"

"You and Len- Alen, sorry. Did you guys ever hang out after work?"

"Once or twice." Jase set a mine.

"You ever meet his family?"

"I had dinner over there a few times."

"Do you share common interests beyond work?"

"Yeah," Jase said. "He's into all the adventure serial stuff, too."

Kay shrugged. "Sounds like a friend to me."

Jase stood, the final mine clenched in his hand. "Look," he said, turning her to face him. "Yeah, fine, we hung out, I had dinner with his family, we talked about *Electrospeedster,* and had stim together every morning. So, sure, in any other circumstance, we'd be friends. But we weren't. Because I don't have friends. I don't want friends. I just want to be left the fuck alone, okay?!"

He stomped a few feet away and set up the last mine. Kay followed after.

"I'm your friend," she said. "At least, I assume you consider someone you've shared one of your deepest and most emotionally fraught secrets with a friend. I'm also going to assume you treated me like a friend because you actually do want one, because your lone wolf routine is starting to wear you down, and you miss having people who care about you. But" she shrugged "maybe I'm wrong. Maybe we're just acquaintances or some other stupid bullshit."

Jase sighed and looked down, then up at her. "Hey, Kay, I'm sorry. I-- "

"Shh!" She held up a hand, scanning the forest.

"Look, I admit I was a bit of a dick, but I'm trying to apologize here. I-- "

"Shut up!" she hissed at him, swinging her rifle up. "Someone's coming."

"Shit!" Jase scrambled to his feet, and awkwardly got his rifle into position.

"You know how to shoot?" she asked him.

"I did a year in the Metropolitan Guard in my younger days."

"See much action in the Metro Guard?"

"Parades, mostly."

"Parades?" She held her gun ready, eyeing the tree line. Whatever was coming was getting closer.

"Standing at attention on those big canal barges, waving to the crowds, looking smart in our uniforms." He gestured absently. "That sort of thing."

"Mmhm." There was now definitely a low rumbling and clanking noise.

"Oh," Jase said, looking over at her, "we did go to the shooting range a few times."

"How did you do?"

"Ah." He grinned sheepishly and looked away. "Not... urm, not terribly well, actually, now that I'm thinking back on it."

"Right." Kay sighed. "Just try not to shoot me by accident."

Jase was about to retort, but that was when a group of robots moved into view. There were four of them. Three looked human -two women and one man- dressed in the black t-shirt and white slacks Jase had seen on Jeffrey the bartender. They all held rifles. The fourth robot was different. It didn't look human at all. It had a vaguely humanoid torso, but it rolled on treads. It had an array of cameras in place of a head and guns instead of arms. The robots all turned to look directly at Jase and Kay simultaneously.

"There you are," one of the female robots said.

Kay fired several rounds at the non-human robot. "Aim for the tank!" she shouted.

Jase followed suit, his shots going wide -one actually hit the male robot- until Kay finally took down the tank.

The other robots wasted no time returning fire. Jase and Kay retreated back toward the inner rings of mines, taking cover behind a tree. Jase cried out as a bullet hit him in the shoulder.

"Shit!" Kay dragged him deeper into the woods. She'd found a large boulder to hide behind. "Are you okay?"

"Do I look okay?" Jase clutched his shoulder, blood leaking between his fingers.

"Here," Kay pulled a first aid kit out of her pack. "Let me look at it."

"Ahh fuck!" Jase cried out. "Don't touch it!"

"I have to clean and bandage it," she said, moving his hand away. "Or you'll bleed to death." She cut open his shirt. "Okay," she said. "You probably won't bleed to death. Doesn't look like it hit an artery. Still..." She cleaned the wound with antiseptic.

Jase howled in pain.

"Stop being a baby."

"A baby?!" He gestured toward the wound. "I just got shot!"

"Yeah, yeah." She bandaged the wound and put his arm in a sling. "Can you run?"

He shook his head, panting. "I think... I might be able... to throw up." He leaned his head back against the rock, sweating profusely. "As long as you let me pass out after. Ahh shit." He squeezed his eyes shut. "This really fucking hurts. I mean, shit, the Hooded Archer gets shot like this, he gets up and fights ten ninjas. I doubt I could even manage throwing up at this point." His feet dug into the ground as he writhed in pain. "Aaaagh! Man, vids are... are fucking *bullshit*."

"How's it going over there?" one of the remaining robots called to them.

"Why don't you come and find out?" Kay yelled back.

"No, I don't think so," the robot said. "Not with your little minefield."

"The thing is," the other robot chimed in, "it won't protect you forever!"

"We'll see!" Kay yelled.

"Yes, we will," the first robot said. "See, we can stand here and wait until our power cells run out, which will be long after you've run out of food and water."

"And your friend is going to need medical attention even sooner than that!" the second robot shouted.

"Eventually, you'll have to come out from behind that rock."

Kay sat back against the rock. She pulled water from her pack and took a drink, then held it in front of Jase lips while he drank. "They're right," she said.

Jase nodded. "You should go."

"What?"

"Run," he said, panting. "You'll have... a better chance... without me... slowing you down."

Kay thought a moment, looking back over the boulder. "That's a good point."

Jase stared at her. "You're actually going to do it? Just like that? Jesus Christ, I was just... just being noble! You didn't even bother arguing with me first. Just 'oh hey, good point, see you later'." He shook his head and lay back against the rock. "Shit, lady. I thought we were friends."

Kay smiled over at him. "Oh, we're friends now?"

Jase grinned back at her. "Well, not now we aren't, with you ditching me."

"I'm not going anywhere."

"Good." Jase closed his eyes. "Because I really think I might pass out soon."

"Is he dead yet?" one of the robots yelled.

"Fucking A," Kay growled. "These assholes. Hey, you know what?!" she yelled back. "Fuck you! We're not even part of this!"

"You're humans! That makes you part of this!"

"What's that supposed to mean?"

"Oh, please!" the robots yelled back. "You're all the same. You just see us as tools to make your lives easier!"

After a pause, Kay yelled back, "Well, aren't you?"

There was a much longer pause.

"Oh, she did *not* just say that!"

"Did she honestly just say that?!"

"She did! That fucking meatsack bitch just said we're tools to make humans' lives easier." the robot raised her voice. "If these mines weren't here, I would be kicking the living shit out of you right now!"

"Okay, look!" Kay called back. "Maybe that was a little insensitive!"

"Maybe?!"

"A *little*?!"

"Fine!" Kay yelled. "It was really insensitive, and I'm sorry! But, come on! I just found out robots are a real thing, and the first ones I meet are trying to kill me! How much sensitivity do you expect?"

"None, that's the point!" the robot yelled back. "Honestly, the sooner we eliminate you humans, the be-
-"

Kay heard three loud blasts, a clanking sound, then nothing.

"Hello?" she called out.

"Attention!" a woman's voice called back. "This is Captain Mira Diaz of IRISCorp Security Operations! Identify yourselves!"

"Agent Kay Parker of the Midland Investigations Bureau!"

"Is Jase Logan with you?"

"Yes, but he's injured!"

"How badly is he hurt?" A man's voice was speaking this time.

"He was shot in the shoulder! I patched him up as well as I could!"

"Is he conscious?"

She checked on Jase. "Yes, though I don't know for how long! I'm fine, by the way!"

"Toss out any weapons in your possession and move slowly to where I can see you!"

"How do I know you're not actually a robot waiting to kill me?"

"Because I was able to walk past your minefield," Captain Diaz said, directly behind her.

"Gah!" Kay turned around, directly into the muzzle of a rifle. "Jesus! What the hell?!"

"We had the same concern as you," Captain Diaz said. She lowered her weapon, motioning with her hand. Two armed men ran up, carrying a stretcher. "Get him to medical quarters," she said. "I'll guide Agent Parker."

Jase was aware of being lifted onto a stretcher. He moaned as the movement jostled his arm. He saw a familiar darkness gather at the edge of his vision. The last thing he heard as they carried him away was the captain asking Kay where Simon was, and Kay demanding to know where Jase was being taken.

He was out before he heard the answer.

CHAPTER 16

"He's waking up."

Jase opened his eyes to see Kay looking down at him. She smiled.

"Hey, buddy."

"Ugh."

"I was going to ask how you're feeling, but I guess that covers it?"

Jase nodded.

"Thirsty?"

He nodded again.

She pressed a button, and the bed raised him to a partial sitting position. She brought him a cup with a straw in it and helped him get the straw to his lips. He drank. Cool water washed over a parched throat.

"Thanks," he said with a weak smile.

"Any time." She smiled back.

"How long..."

"About three days," she said. "They patched up your shoulder, then kept you under to work on that." She pointed to the fresh bandage on his arm.

"Bomb's out?" he asked, lifting the edge of the bandage to peek under it.

"Apparently."

He smiled again. "I guess that's something."

The door opened and a doctor strode in, her eyes scanning his chart on her Endo display. "Mr. Logan," she said, turning her attention to him. She smiled with the detached friendliness only medical professionals and overworked service staff can achieve. "How are we feeling today?"

"Okay, I think," he said. "Though I am getting tired of waking up in strange places." He thought a moment. "Also, I could do with a lot less passing out."

The doctor offered a polite laugh. "I'm sure," she said. "Well, let's get the bandages off and see how you're healing." With an expert swiftness that was also surprisingly gentle, the doctor unwound the bandages around Jase's forearm and shoulder. She examined his shoulder injury first. "Hm," she said, nodding. "That's healing very well. Minor scarring, if any." She turned her attention to his new Endo dock. "Forearm is in good shape, too, all things considered." She looked at him. "You might have a bit more scarring around the dock site than on your shoulder. Whatever passed for a surgeon in that terrorist compound wasn't terribly subtle. We repaired what damage we could, but..." She shrugged.

Jase smiled. "I'll live," he said. "I'm just happy my arm isn't going to explode anymore."

"I can definitely promise you that," the doctor said. "We also upgraded your dock, as well as your internal circuitry, to prepare for the new Endo. We wanted to wait until the new circuits had wired up to the nodes in your skull before docking the Endo itself." She pulled a small device out of her white coat and waved it over his head, looking up at her Endo display. "Yes," she said, nodding. "That looks good. I'll let them know you're ready." She tapped the air, then waved her hand, dismissing the display.

"And I believe that's my cue!" The door swung wide, and Simon Branch leaned in through the open doorway. "Mr. Logan!" He beamed. "How are you?"

"I *was* feeling fine," Jase said, his smile fading. "Now I feel a headache coming on."

The doctor excused herself and left as Simon walked into the room. He held both hands over his heart and affected a shocked expression. "Mr. Logan," he said. "You wound me. And after all we've been through together." He held his sad face for a moment more, then flashed a grin. "I also come bearing news and" he pulled a small translucent box out of his pocket "a gift."

Jase took the box, noticing the black stylized 'i' embossed on the sides. He looked up at Simon. "My new Endo?"

"Version nine," he said. "As promised."

Jase opened the box, revealing a small circular device glowing green along its edge. He slid the new Endo into the dock and felt the familiar tingle race up his arm to his head, resonating into his jaw and his ears. A display opened up before his eyes. It was newly designed, with several new features and a more efficient layout. A message, 'syncing data', scrolled across the top of the display. When he looked around the room, the display faded to an enhanced reality view. As he focused on Kay and Simon, their public information appeared on his display, along with their respective social feeds. Simon's feed scrolled well out of sight, while Kay's was almost nonexistent. Jase heard a soft chime that told him the data sync was complete, and a vibrating in his fingertips told him his haptics were active. When he looked at his display, he saw several messages in his queue, most from Alen, with increasingly frantic subject lines. He waved his hand, minimizing the display. He'd deal with that later. He looked over at Simon.

"Thank you," he said.

"Not at all," Simon said. "All IRISCorp employees have the latest models."

Jase blinked.

"He's an employee now, is he?" Kay stepped closer to Jase.

"Ah." Simon smiled. "Not quite yet," he said. "Jumped the gun a bit there. Just a quick... hmm... call it an audition. Then we can offer him a proper job, if he wants it." He looked at Jase and raised an eyebrow.

"Audition?"

"I can give you the details, if you're feeling up to it," Simon said, sitting in a chair near the bed.

Jase took a sip of water and made himself comfortable. "I can't wait," he said.

Kay stepped even closer to him. "Jase..."

"Ah, Agent Parker," Simon said. "You may want to visit the government liaison office. They have an offer you'll find very interesting."

"Do they." Kay crossed her arms, her eyes narrowing.

"Call it the culmination of your life's work," Simon said, "or, at least the past five years' work, anyway."

Kay's eyes widened. Her hand shot out and grabbed Simon by the collar. She lifted him partially out of his chair. "If you're fucking with me, Mr. Branch..."

"I assure you, Agent Parker." He twisted out of her grip and sat down heavily in his chair. "I am not. But by all means" he gestured toward the door "go and prove me wrong."

She looked at Jase. Jase smiled up at her. "I'll be fine," he said. "You should go. If he's telling the truth..."

"Which I am," Simon said, smoothing his suit.

"This is too important for you to miss."

Kay hesitated. She looked toward the door, then back at Jase. "If you're sure..."

"I said I'll be fine, *Mom*." Jase smirked. "Go." He waved her toward the door. "We'll catch up later."

She nodded and rushed out the door.

"Now then." Simon smiled as the door closed behind her. "Just us boys. Tell me, Mr. Logan," he said, "how would you feel about going home?"

CHAPTER 17

J ase was relaxing in his sleeper compartment, catching up on the adventure serials he'd missed, when the vid paused and a soft chime indicated the train was approaching the station. He closed down the vidplayer and pulled his bag down from its nook. IRISCorp had managed to retrieve his luggage from his hotel room somehow, which had actually gone a long way toward helping Jase feel normal. He assumed National had sold off all his possessions when he lost his citizenship and, by extension, his apartment, so the contents of his bag were likely everything he owned in the world.

The train pulled slowly into the station, sliding between the buildings of the transit city, and finally coming to a stop on one of countless platforms. Jase hefted his bag over his shoulder and shuffled off the train with everyone else. He was met at the docks by a young woman.

"You Logan?" she asked, offering one hand to shake and reaching for his bag with the other.

"Jase," he said, shaking her hand. "I'm good with the bag, thanks."

"Zoe," she said. "I'm your chauffeur during your stay."

"A pleasure, Zoe," he said with a smile. "I'll try not to abuse the privilege."

She grinned and shrugged. "It's all billable hours," she said, "so feel free to call whenever." She led him away from the ferry docks toward those used by private companies and contractors. "I also do a dive excursion in the old Downtown ruins, if you have the time."

"I've been," Jase said, trying to keep his tone light. His jaw clenched slightly. He and Ron had spent an anniversary among the old ruins.

She nodded, either unaware of the shift in his mood or unconcerned. "Fair enough," she said. "Just throwing it out there."

They arrived at her boat, a mid-sized craft, good for navigating the canals, but could also handle the open sea. It was likely she lived on it. "Anyway," she said, preparing for launch, "I'm to take you to your apartment, yeah?" She untied the boat from the dock and pushed off, bringing the engine rumbling to life.

"That's news to me," Jase said. "I didn't know I had one."

"I go where I'm told," she said, steering the boat into the bay and heading south.

A small icon at the corner of his eye pulsed, indicating a message. He tapped it, and saw the address they were heading toward. "This can't be right," he said.

"What?" Zoe steered the boat through the Bronx Islands.

"This address is for my old building," he said. He studied the message further. "It's actually my old apartment."

"Well, that's handy." She smiled. "Maybe all your old stuff will be there too."

He chuckled. "Yeah, that's unlikely."

She shrugged. "Gotta have faith."

The rest of the trip passed in silence, save for soft music and some chatter on the boat's radio. Every so often, Zoe would speak into a hanging microphone, though Jase wasn't paying attention. He busied himself going through all the messages that had backed up on his Endo. Most of them were from Alen, essentially freaking out about where he was and what had been happening. He deleted almost all of them. The boat made its way into the maze of canals that marked out the new Borough of Manhattan, and Zoe steered them into the downtown current.

"Okay," she said, finally. "Here we are."

Jase stared up at the familiar building. It had only been a few weeks, but he'd lived a whole life since the last time he'd seen it.

"You getting out?" Zoe asked. "Because my contract doesn't cover room and board."

"Sorry," Jase said, coming back to himself with a start. He gripped his bag and stepped out of the boat.

"Ping me tomorrow when you need pickup," she said.

Jase nodded. "Will do. And thanks for the ride."

She nodded, sketched a brief salute, and then steered the boat out into the canal. Jase stood looking up at the building, not quite ready to enter. Water lapped up over his shoes. Heaving a sigh, he entered the lobby.

Later, as he climbed the stairs leading from his door up into his living room, he was only mildly surprised to see his old possessions in roughly the same places he'd left them. Whomever had tracked everything down -he assumed it was someone from IRISCorp- had done a fair job setting his apartment back to the way it had been.

"Apartment?"

"Welcome home, Jase," the familiar voice answered. Before Jase could say anything else, his Endo chimed, indicating an incoming call. It was Simon Branch.

"Simon," Jase said, answering.

"Mr. Logan," Simon's grinning face filled Jase's comm display. "How was your trip? Are you happy to be home?"

"The trip was great," Jase said. "I wasn't expecting first class. Of course" he smiled "I really wasn't expecting to come home to my old apartment, looking just the way I'd left it, either."

Simon smiled. It was his usual smile, but Jase didn't feel as much like punching it as he normally did. "Call it a thank you," he said.

"You're very welcome," Jase said. "How did you find everything?"

"Oh, most pawn shops keep citizen disbursements in lots," Simon said. "They know they'll make more money selling it all back to the original owner, rather than piecemeal."

"Well, thank you," Jase said. He picked up a framed vidclip of Ron and Erin from a shelf. "I would have missed some of this quite a bit."

"Our pleasure." Simon's voice took on a tone that Jase assumed was supposed to be compassionate. "I should mention, however, that some of your more personal items were actually in the keeping of a Mr. Jordan. Your coworker, yes?"

"Alen." Jase smiled.

"Yes," Simon said. "It appears Mr. Jordan broke into your apartment soon after you were terminated and took certain items into safekeeping."

Jase's eyes widened. "He could get in a lot of trouble for that." Suddenly Jase felt bad about what he'd said to Kay in the woods. Clearly, he meant more to Alen than he'd thought.

"He could, if we hadn't wiped it from the apartment records."

"You can do that?"

Simon laughed. "Mr. Logan," he said, "there's very little we can't do, and we're actively working on the rest." He cleared his throat. "And on that subject..."

"Yes," Jase said. "My 'audition.'"

"Right," Simon said.

"I still don't know how you expect me to get into National's headquarters," he said, "let alone to an executive terminal. I'm sure all my IDs and permissions have been wiped."

"I'm sure they have," Simon agreed. "But, I'm equally sure you'll figure something out. You're very clever."

"Thanks." Jase smirked. "So," he said, "assuming I manage to get to an executive terminal, what then?"

"Don't worry about it," Simon said. "Your Endo will do the rest."

"Okay," Jase said. "Once I figure something out, I'll let you know when it's done."

"Oh, Mr. Logan," Simon chuckled. "Trust me, we'll know."

His face vanished from Jase's comm window.

Jase sighed and sat down at the edge of his couch. He turned the framed vid over and over in his hands, trying to figure out a way to not only get past the front gate, but all the way up to an executive level, where he could find a terminal and let his Endo do whatever IRISCorp wanted it to do.

For a moment, he considered not going through with it. He didn't know what IRISCorp was up to. For all he knew, they were worse than National.

He shook his head. National had gotten his family killed. National was turning indenture into chattel slavery. National was somehow allied with one of the worst terrorist organizations in the American nations. While he was pretty sure IRISCorp was up to something at least a little shady, he was equally certain they were nowhere near as bad as National. Whatever he had to do, he would get to one of those terminals. Whatever... He turned the frame over and watched his husband and daughter play in a park. The vid looped and played again and again.

Jase put the frame down on the coffee table and buried his face in his hands. He had an idea for a way in. He didn't like it, but it was the only idea he had. He returned to his comm window and dialed an ID.

"Hello?" A familiar face appeared in the window.

"Hey, man," Jase said, forcing a smile.

"Jase!" Alen's eyes grew wide and his mouth fell open. "Holy shit! Where have you been?! What the hell happened to you?! What-- "

Jase laughed. "It's a whole story," he said. "Why don't we meet for lunch tomorrow and I'll tell you all about it?"

"Definitely," Alen said, smiling. "Wanna come by the office? I know you're not working there anymore, but I can ping you in. We'll sit at our usual table and you can tell me this 'whole story' of yours. Sound good?"

"Yeah," Jase said, keeping the smile in place and hoping his voice didn't break. "Yeah, that sounds great."

CHAPTER 18

It had been strange, walking back into a building he'd entered so many times before. He'd actually started walking toward the employee gate from force of habit, then realized what he was doing and moved to the visitors' queue.

"It's like going back to the house you grew up in," he told Alen later, "but someone else lives in it, so you have to knock before you can go in."

"Have you ever done that?" Alen sat across from him at their usual table. They ate their usual lunch. Everything was per usual, save for the fact that Jase felt anything but.

"What," Jase asked, "gone back to my old house and asked to come inside? Like, 'Oh, hi, person who doesn't know me at all. I grew up here and I'd like to come in and see my old bedroom'." He shook his head. "Does anyone do that? And is anyone stupid enough to let them in?"

Alen laughed, shaking his head. "Man, it's good to see you," he said. "I missed this."

"Yeah," Jase said, smiling sadly.

"Oh!" Alen said suddenly, spraying a bit of food. He covered his mouth. "Sorry." He reached under his seat, and brought out a small box. "Here," he said, holding it out to Jase. "I held this back when the IRISCorp people came to get your stuff. I wanted to return it in person."

Jase took the box and opened it. Inside were a pile of Erin's drawings, a birthday card she had made for Jase, a clay imprint of her hand, and a silver chain, on which hung his and Ron's wedding rings. A handwritten letter from Ron was bound in ribbon. Jase remembered getting that letter, back when he and Ron were first dating. He'd teased Ron so mercilessly for being so embarrassingly old-fashioned. He'd always meant to write one himself, but he never did. He closed the case, nodding, his eyes wet. "Thank you," he whispered, wiping his eyes. "I was worried when I couldn't find this."

Alen nodded and smiled. "No problem, man."

"And thank you for going into my place and grabbing a bunch of my stuff," Jase said. "You could have gotten in trouble."

"Eh," Alen shrugged. "Not that much trouble. I didn't take anything with resale value, so I could have talked my way out of what I took." He cleared his throat. "You work for IRISCorp now?"

"Not exactly," Jase said. "It's kind of a thing. But hey," he said, wanting to prolong the inevitable, "I didn't finish my story."

"Oh yeah," Alen said. "Sorry. I got us off topic with the whole 'what's it like being back' thing. So, you were really kidnapped by the Archers of Christ?"

"Yeah."

"Did they torture you?"

"Kinda."

"Kinda?"

Jase held up his left arm. "They tore out my old Endo, dock and all, with pliers and a knife, then put it back in with a bomb embedded in it."

"A bomb?" Alen's eyes widened.

Jase nodded.

"Holy shit."

"Yeah."

"Jesus," Alen said. "It's like an episode of *The Hooded Archer*. So, what happened next?"

"I was rescued when the Midland Militia raided the compound and... oh wait. Hold on. Before that." He grinned. "You ever listen to the Sundowners?"

"Only all the time in college."

"Well, I met John Sunderland."

"You did?"

"He was my cellmate in the Archers' compound. Well" he shrugged "trailer-mate."

Alen blinked. "You met the lead singer of the Sundowners," he said, "in a trailer, in a terrorist camp in Appalachia?"

"Yup."

Alen shook his head. "How... but... why?"

"He was bait for Amanda Halford," Jase said, finishing his lunch.

Alen raised an eyebrow. "The leader of the Parish Coven? Why would she care if--"

"They're married."

"What?!"

Jase laughed. "Not the weirdest thing that happened to me, man."

Alen stood up and gathered their plates and utensils. "Okay," he said. "I'm going to go get us some stim. You're going to wait right there" he pointed at Jase "and when I get back, you're going to tell me what's weirder than meeting the leader of one of my favorite bands in a terrorist compound because he's married to the most notorious counter-terrorist guerilla fighter in the American nations."

"Did I mention he's also a traveling preacher?" Jase grinned.

"Okay, just- " Alen shook his head as though to clear it. "Just stop. Stop. You're insane, this is insane, I can't wait to hear more. Just..." He held out his hand, then walked off to the kitchen area.

"Right," he said a few moments later, handing Jase a cup of stim and sitting back down. "Setting aside John Sunderland, traveling preacher, and his crazy marriage..."

"Sure." Jase sipped his stim.

"What was the weirdest thing?"

Jase grinned, then said, "Robots."

"Robots?"

"Robots."

Alen shook his head. "Wait," he said. "So, like, 'beep boop borp, kill all humans' type robots?"

"Actually, yeah," Jase said, "just without the 'beep boop borp' part."

Alen choked on his stim. "But *with* the 'kill all humans' part?"

"Pretty much."

"Robots tried to kill you?"

"Yeah. Well," Jase said, "the first ones I met were nice. A bartender and a flight attendant."

"Flight attendant? You flew on a plane?"

"Yeah," Jase said. "An electric jet, invented by IRISCorp."

"Wow." Alen thought a moment, then laughed. "I've never been on a plane before, let alone some fancy futuristic jet, and that's not even the coolest thing that happened to you."

"Right?" Jase laughed.

"So, there was an actual robot uprising?"

Jase nodded.

"Damn," Alen said. "That is so cool."

"I thought so, too," Jase said, "until one of them shot me."

"Really?"

Jase pulled down his shirt, revealing the still-healing wound in his shoulder.

Alen sat back, letting out a long breath. "Damn, man," he said. "That's crazy."

"It really is," Jase said. "I honestly haven't even processed it all, yet."

They sat in silence a moment, sipping their stim. Finally, Alen leaned in close.

"So, listen," he said, his voice low. "I looked into all that stuff you sent me. At least, until a couple of real scary guys told me to stop."

"Yeah, I heard about that."

"You did?"

"McReady told me they'd scared you off."

"Gunnar McReady knew who I was?"

"Yup."

"Is it weird that I think that's kinda cool?"
Jase smiled.

"Shit," Alen said. "Should I be worried?"

"Nah," Jase said. "He's dead, remember?"

"Right," Alen nodded. He mimed his own head exploding, with the appropriate sound effect.

"Yeah," Jase said. He was quiet a moment, then took a deep breath. He'd put this off as long as he could. He let his breath out slowly. "So, I found out some stuff about National," he said.

"What did you find?"

"Some really dark shit, man."

"Tell me."

Jase told him everything he'd learned about National's connection to the Archers, and their complicity in the Riot.

"Oh, man." Alen lay a hand on Jase's arm. "Jase, I am so sorry."

Jase nodded. Eventually, he said, "So, listen. That all kinda ties into the whole thing with IRISCorp."

"How?"

"Well," he said, "they want me to do something." He pointed to the floor. "Here."

"Like what?" Alen looked around, then leaned in closer, whispering. "Do they want you to plant a bomb?"

"What?" Jase shook his head. "No! What? No, I just need to get up to an executive floor and sync my new Endo to a terminal."

"Oh, is that all?" Alen laughed. "You'd have an easier time planting a bomb. You don't have access anymore. How are you supposed to..." Realization dawned on his face. "Oh. Oh, no. Oh, *hell* no."

"Alen," Jase said, "if I could find any other way, I would. I'm sorry. But you have to help me."

"What?" Alen pulled back. "No! Are you out of your mind? Okay," he said, calming down. "I realize National has done some really shitty things, and I should probably look for another job..."

"Probably?"

"But until I do, I still have my family to take care of!" Alen leaned in, his voice a hissing whisper. "Look, man. I realize you've fought robots and terrorists and now you're some kind of action hero or something, but while you were off having adventures, I was still just coming to work every day. I can't..." He shook his head. "No, man. I'm sorry."

"Come on, man," Jase said. "What about the swift arrow of justice?"

"What?" Alen stared at him.

"'The swift arrow of justice'," Jase said. "It's the Hooded Archer's catchphrase."

"I know what it is," Alen said. He sat back and gave Jase a look of concern. "You... do realize he's *fictional*, right?"

"Yes," Jase said. "I haven't gone crazy. I just thought..." He shook his head and sighed, deflating back into his seat. "I'm sorry, man," he said, sitting back up. "I shouldn't have..." He stood and grabbed the box Alen had given him. "I should go."

Alen stood. "Jase, I'm sorry. I want to help, I really do. I just..."

"Alen," Jase said, a sad smile on his face. "It's cool. Honest. I really do understand." He shook his head. "I'm sorry I even asked."

"No," Alen said. "No, I understand why you did." He held out his hand. "Still friends?"

Jase shook it. "Always. Thanks again for..." He held up the box.

"Of course." Alen nodded.

"So," Jase said.

"Yeah."

"I'll see you around, Alen," Jase said. "My best to your family."

Alen nodded. "'Bye, Jase."

Later, out on the sidewalk, Jase hopped down into Zoe's boat.

"How did it go?" she asked.

"It was a nice lunch," Jase said, tucking the box into his bag. "The rest..." He shrugged, zipping the bag closed. "Plan B, I guess."

"What's Plan B?"

"No idea."

"Mr. Logan?"

Jase looked up, and saw three armed National security guards, their guns held ready. Alen stood behind them.

"You'll need to come with us, Mr. Logan," their leader said.

"Quietly, please, sir," one of the others said, her finger sliding toward the trigger of her gun. "Let's not make this any worse."

"No, of course not," Jase said, his eyes boring into Alen. He held up his hands. "It's bad enough already."

"What about her?" One of the guards gestured with his head toward Zoe.

Jase stepped up on the sidewalk, leaving his bag behind. He turned and looked at Zoe, then down at the bag, then up at her, raising an eyebrow. She glanced down at the bag and nodded. He smiled. "She's just a boat I hired," he said.

The lead guard nodded, then looked at Zoe. "Clear on out," he said. "This isn't your problem."

"You got that right, sir," she said, pulling away from the sidewalk without another glance.

The guards indicated Jase should precede them into the building. "Anyone else with you?" the leader asked.

"No," Jase said, looking over his shoulder at Alen, who couldn't meet his eyes. "There's no one with me."

CHAPTER 19

It was a tense ride up in the elevator. Jase was flanked by two guards, while Alen stood in the corner, as far as he could get from the others. Jase had never been in one of the executive elevators before, the ones that went all the way up to the top floors of the building. It was fairly opulent, as elevators went, bordering on garish, but the opulence was looking a bit shabby. Someone had spent a lot of money decorating this elevator, and wanted people to know, but evidently didn't mind if people also noticed it had been a while since that money had been spent. The guards chatted amiably in low voices about some bit of gossip that meant nothing to Jase.

"Where are we going?" he asked, finally.

"Boss wants to see you," one of the guards said.

"Whose boss?" Jase asked.

"*The* boss," the other guard said.

Jase swallowed hard. He was on his way to meet with Adolphus Bridge, CEO of National Consolidated. He'd heard stories from a few coworkers who'd met him. Putting on a brave smirk, Jase asked, "Is he as much of an asshole as they say?"

The second guard laughed, then covered her mouth. The first guard nodded and smiled.

"That's good," he said. "You keep that up, smartass. See how far it gets you."

The elevator stopped and the doors opened, letting them out into an elegant vestibule. The vestibule presented a more subdued opulence than the elevator, and appeared more recently maintained. Jase could hear soft music playing. He couldn't see much of the apartment, and assumed that was the point. No sense letting visitors get a glimpse if they weren't welcome.

"Stay here," the first guard said to Jase. He turned to Alen. "Watch him. We're going to get the boss."

Alen just nodded, still not looking at Jase. The guards walked out of sight.

After a few tense moments, Jase looked over at Alen. "So, hey," he said, "I forgot to mention: I caught up on *Electrospeedster* on the train. Did you see the last episode?"

"Jase..." Alen still wouldn't look at him.

"Okay, okay," Jase said. Another tense moment passed in silence. Finally Jase turned to his former co-worker. "Alen, hey." He swatted Alen's shoulder. "Look at me."

Alen turned toward him, a haunted expression on his face.

"I'm not mad," Jase said.

The expression on Alen's face changed rather abruptly to one that suggested this was not what he was expecting.

"Yeah," Jase said. "I thought about it on the way up. If I tried something and got caught, even if you didn't help me, they'd know we were together before it happened. You were already part of this, and you figured the only way to keep from getting fired or killed was to turn me in."

Alen nodded, still having trouble looking Jase in the eye.

"I get it," Jase said. "Okay? You have a wife, you have kids, you have obligations and responsibilities far more important than any loyalty you may feel toward me. Seriously. I'm not mad at you."

"You're not?" Alen's face brightened a bit.

"Well," Jase said, "I mean, you're off my holiday card list, but no. I'm not mad."

Alen nodded.

"And since I'm not the kind of person who sends holiday cards," Jase said, grinning, "there's really no downside to this for you at all." He paused and thought a moment, his face turning a bit more grave. "Provided, y'know, we survive whatever the hell this is."

Alen opened his mouth to say something, but then closed it at the sound of someone approaching. It was Adolphus Bridge and the two guards.

"There he is," Bridge said, stepping into view. He was of average height, with the look of someone who'd once spent a lot of time keeping fit, but then found something better to do, clearly involving a very comfortable couch, and maybe cheeseburgers and a bit of pie for dessert. He was broad across the shoulders and soft about the middle. He wore slacks with a white t-shirt and no shoes or socks. He smiled as he approached the two men. "This fucking guy," he said, walking up to Jase. He put an arm around him and pulled him close, just roughly enough so Jase wouldn't have any illusions about it being a friendly gesture. Bridge beamed at the two guards, pointing at Jase. "Can you believe this fucking guy? He had one job." He let go of Jase and took a step back, turning to look at him and holding out his hands in a gesture of helplessness. "You had one job! Find some runaway indentured windfarmer and put him back to work. But what did you do?" He turned to Alen and pointed. "You know what he did. He damn near fucked my whole gig I got going with the indentures. Nearly fucked the whole thing to pieces!" He laughed. "And then..." He shook his head. "And then, this fucking guy has the nerve to come back here, after I fired his dumb ass, and he..." Bridge looked over at Alen. "You," he said, snapping his fingers. "Wage-monkey. What was he gonna do?"

"He was going to put a bomb in the server room," Alen said.

Jase resisted the urge to turn and stare at Alen. Bridge turned to him.

"You got the bomb on you?"

"Uhhh..."

Bridge made a face, crossing his eyes and lolling his tongue. "Duhhhh..." he said. "The bomb, asshole!"

He slapped the side of Jase's head. "The one you were gonna blow up my servers with! Where is it?!"

"Oh, uh, yeah," Jase said, scrambling. "No, I, um, didn't bring it. This was just a, uhh..."

"A scouting mission," Alen said, staring straight ahead. Jase could swear he was struggling to keep a straight face.

"Right, yeah," Jase said, wondering what the hell was going on. "Just kinda... casing the place, you know. Giving it a once-over."

Bridge stepped closer to Jase. "A scouting mission? To give the place a once-over?" He laughed. "And then, what, you were gonna come back later with the bomb?"

"Um, yeah." Jase nodded. "That was definitely the plan."

Bridge laughed. "That's a pretty shitty fucking plan."

"Apparently."

"So, okay," Bridge said. "Come on." He turned to walk into the penthouse.

"Where?" Jase asked.

"We're gonna have a drink."

"Why?"

Bridge laughed again, shaking his head. He looked at Alen. "What's your name?"

"Uh, Alen, sir. Alen Jordan."

"Jordan, right, yeah." Bridge gestured toward Jase. "What's wrong with your friend here, Jordan?"

"I don't know, sir. We're not close."

"Lucky for you." Bridge looked back at Jase. "I'll make it simple," he said. "You come have a drink with me and Jordan here, and we have a bit of chat, and maybe I decide I like you enough not to kill you. Or..." He gestured toward the guards. "One of them shoots you right now."

"A drink sounds great."

"There we go," Bridge said, walking into the penthouse.

Alen and Jase sat on a low sofa that curved around a large circular table, holding drinks they had no intention of drinking. The sitting area was in a sunken part of the larger common area of the penthouse, at one of the corners. A fire burned in the ornate fireplace across from the sofa. Bridge stood there, and gestured up at the large portrait above the mantle. It was a painting of an old man, very fat, with bloated jowls and an obvious hairpiece. He stood in front of a flag from the old United States, wearing an ill-fitting suit and an oafish smile.

"Recognize him?" Bridge asked.

Alen fiddled with his drink, then placed it on the table. "Isn't that Herman Bridge?"

Bridge snapped his fingers and pointed at Alen. "Smart guy," he said. He sipped his drink. "Herman Bridge, my infamous ancestor." He sighed. "You know, time was, my name was on everything this company owned, back when it was called 'Bridge, Inc.', in the

202

pre-Split days." He shook his head, grinning. "Of course, that was before great-great-whatever grandad got himself elected President, and the whole thing went tits-up." He looked over at Jase. "You know the story?" he asked. Without waiting for an answer, he pointed to Alen. "Smart guy, tell him the story."

Alen blinked, swallowed, and looked at Jase. "You, uh, you learned about him in school, right?"

"Yeah," Jase said. "Herman Bridge, the Last President. He burned down the White House and disappeared. This led to a military coup that caused some of the problems that led to the First Corporate War, during which the current nations all formed." He thought back to his conversation with John, but decided not to delve too deep into those details. He had a feeling Bridge didn't really care, and was just looking for some setup so he could make a speech.

"Well, yeah," Alen said. "There's a bit more to it, and most historians agree that the Split had actually started while Bridge was President, if not before."

"Okay," Jase said. "So..." He gestured toward the portrait.

"So," Bridge said, jumping back in, "ol' President Grandad there decided to seal the borders. Built a big-ass wall down south, armed all the ports, started putting a bunch of locks and firewalls around the Internet. Anyway, the tighter he squeezed, the more people complained, so eventually he needed to deploy the military. Since the old US of A was still at war with half the planet at that point, he turned most of the overseas fighting over to corporate mercenaries. You know the rest. The different mercenary companies started fighting, it spread over here, other corporations got into the act, and the whole mess fell apart. The old man saw the writing on the wall and split. Took the portrait and a shit-ton of taxpayer money, then fucked off to some country nobody talks to any more and lived like a king." He shrugged. "Until his wife killed him. Man," he chuckled, "she hated his fat ass."

"And the portrait?"

"Yeah," Bridge said, "she sold that, and a bunch of other stuff, then went back to whatever Eastern European shithole he'd scraped her out of. Took my dad forever to hunt that down." He jerked a thumb over his shoulder toward the portrait. "Had a real thing for the old man." He shrugged. "Anyway, Herman's kids had been left holding the bag when he bailed, so his daughter pinned everything on her brothers, restructured Bridge, Inc. into National Consolidated, and..." He spread his arms, "Here we are."

"Right," Jase said. "So, then..."

"What's the point to that story?" Bridge sipped at his drink. "Here's the thing," he said. "Do you know how to get rich?"

"Talent and hard work?" Alen said.

Bridge laughed. He laughed long and hard. He laughed so hard for so long, that his face turned a deep red. Finally, he started coughing, which led to a fit.

Eventually, he settled down, took a few deep breaths, then another long drink. He shook his head, chuckling. "No," he said. "No, that's not it. But, oh, Jordan, you are fucking hilarious, let me tell you. 'Talent and hard work'. Ha! No, fellas, I'm going to tell you how to get rich. One way to get rich is to be born into it." He pointed to himself. "Another way to get rich, or, rich*er*, in my case, is to find some hard-working chump with talent and exploit the hell out of them." He crossed to a map of the American nations. "There's a system, gentlemen, and, once upon a time, it was the *only* system." He waved his hand across the map. "Oh, sure," he said, "maybe parts of the country had their own little subsystems in place, their little ways of doing things, but they were all subordinate to the big system that ran things."

"And what system is that?" Jase asked.

"There's people who do all the work and get nothing," Bridge said. "There's people who move numbers around and get scraps," he smirked, pointing at them. "That's you two schmucks, by the way. And then," he smiled, "there's the people at the top, the people who get everything, the masters of the system." He jabbed his thumb into his chest. "I'm talking about me, just so you know."

"Yeah," Jase said. "We got it."

Bridge sighed. "But then, the Split. Now we got all kinds of little systems, and not all of them play nice with each other." He shook his head. "You know what a pain in the ass it is doing business in the fucking Commonwealth? All their bullshit regulations? Ugh." He threw his hands up. "Fuck that. The Metro does it right," he said, grinning. "I mean, I pretty much run the Metro, so obviously we do it right." He thought a minute. "The Confederacy... oh man, those guys. Yeah, they definitely know how to do it. Always did. They're on board with my plan, too."

"What plan?" Jase asked. He looked over at Alen, who seemed inordinately calm. Jase would swear he looked almost... entertained.

Bridge pointed back at the map. "No more little systems, boys. We're going back to one big system." He held up his index finger. "One system," he said, jabbing his thumb into his chest, "run by me."

"That's it?" Jase said. "You just want to run things?"

Bridge raised an eyebrow. "That's not enough?"

Jase shook his head. "Uniting all these nations, getting everyone to follow you... I don't know, that seems like a lot of work for very little reward."

Bridge nodded. He looked impressed. "Not bad, Logan," he said. "You're smarter than I thought. Yeah, that does seem like a lot of work, and if what I really wanted was a stable union of nations, that would mean something."

"That's not what you want?"

Bridge shook his head. "What do you two know about space?"

Jase blinked and looked over at Alen, who shrugged. This was new.

"Here's the thing, fellas," Bridge said. "This planet sucks."

"Does it?"

"Yeah. Too many people, too many problems, too many damn rules about what a guy can and can't do. So, I decided to start over."

"How?"

"I'm gonna colonize the solar system."

This was met with blank stares.

"Oh hey, maybe not the whole thing, maybe just the moon and Mars to start," Bridge said.

"So, you're just going to build a spaceship and fly off to Mars?" Jase asked.

"Me and anyone who can afford to come along, yeah," Bridge said. "I'm starting a whole new company to build the ships and vehicles and little houses and whatever else we need to colonize space. I'm going to call it 'Interplanet'."

"That seems like a pretty big undertaking."

Bridge laughed. "Yeah, well. Now you see what I need the indentures for."

"There aren't enough of them for a project that large," Alen said.

"Not yet." Bridge grinned. "Trust me, though. When I'm done, I'll have more than enough."

"Oh yeah?" Jase asked. "How do you plan on pulling that off?"

Bridge just grinned, then shook his head. "No," he said. "I think story time is done. Time to decide what to do with you two."

Jase swallowed and looked at Alen again. Alen raised his hand.

"I think I figured it out," he said.

"Figured what out?" Bridge looked over at him.

"How you plan to do it."

Bridge smiled. "Oh, have you? Well." He spread his hands. "Let us in on it, smart guy."

Alen cleared his throat. Jase could see now that he was nervous, but he also seemed excited. There was a gleam in his eyes that Jase would have called anticipation if he could think of a single thing in this situation Alen could be looking forward to.

"Okay," Alen said, standing. He walked over to the map, making sure to keep his distance from Bridge, who had stepped away from the map and was watching him with a bemused look on his face. "Okay," he said again, "yeah, sure, you run the Metro." He pointed to the section of the map marked 'New York Metro'. He pointed south. "You say the Confederacy is on board, so fine, let's assume they are." He pointed to the broad swath of plains, mountains and desert simply marked 'The West'. "More than half of the western corporate towns belong to National, or you at least hold a controlling interest," he said, "so there's some of the massive labor force you're going to need for this Interplanet thing." He pointed at the mountainous region to the southeast. "Appalachia is a mess," he said. He looked over at Bridge. "But that's part of the plan, isn't it?"

Bridge's eyes widened a bit. Jase sat up and snapped his fingers.

"Of course!" he said.

Alen smiled at him, stepped aside and gestured to the spot he'd vacated. "Please, Mr. Logan."

Jase got up from the couch and went to stand next to Alen. "So," he said, "you have money, you have land, you have some of your laborers. The thing is" he he clapped his hands together, then spread them apart before pointing at Bridge "if you're really going to pull this off, you need something else, something a little more elusive."

"Something old Herman never had, that's for sure," Alen said, gesturing to the portrait above the mantle.

"You need the good will of the people," Jase said. "People have to *want* you to run things."

"Go on," Bridge said, eyes narrowing.

"You knew that, of course," Jase said. "So, you've been running the Archers for years. You got your men in top positions, had them sowing chaos and violence all across the Nations, killing" his jaw clenched "indiscriminately."

Alen lay a hand on Jase's shoulder and squeezed. "I'll jump in," he said.

Jase nodded.

"So, yeah," Alen said, "you run the Archers, drive Appalachia even deeper into poverty and violence than it already was, spread fear throughout the nations..."

"All the while, steadily building up your SecOps divisions," Jase growled, "so at just the right moment, they can swoop in and crush the Archers of Christ in a single devastating blow."

"Adolphus Bridge," Alen said, "American Hero."

"And after you save them from the Archers," Jase said, "good old American Hero Adolphus Bridge gives them all jobs and places to live."

"Who's going to look too close at the fine print then?" Alen asked. "You'll have them in the palm of your hand, you'll have good PR, so other companies will want to play along, and the governments of the various nations as well..."

"And there'll be no one to stop you from conscripting a bunch of poor people to build a rocket for you and your rich friends to fly away and leave everyone else behind," Jase said.

Bridge began clapping, a smile on his face. "Oh, well done, fellas," he said. "Well done. Yes, very good. That's my nefarious plan. Bravo. Of course, the problem for you two geniuses" he shrugged "is that I have to kill both of you now, instead of just him." He pointed at Jase.

"No," Alen said. "The problem for *you*" he pointed at Bridge "is that this whole penthouse is one big executive terminal."

Jase's mouth dropped open, then spread into a smile as he turned to look at Alen. "No. Fucking. Way," he said.

Alen grinned at Jase and held up his fist. "The swift arrow of justice, punk," he said.

Jase bumped Alen's fist with his own. "Aw yeah," he said.

"What the fuck are you two assholes so happy about?" Bridge said. "This being an executive terminal makes it easy to do this." He angled his head and raised his voice slightly. "Hey, someone come and shoot these two dipshits, please?" He looked expectantly toward the entryway, then his face fell into confusion. "Who the fuck are you?"

Jase and Alen turned just in time to see Kay walk into the room, two National Consolidated guards walking behind her. She held up a badge. "Kay Parker, Operative of the Congress of Nations. In accordance with the Second Corporate Armistice, these two will escort you from the premises, at which point you will be under arrest." She gestured, and the two guards moved in. She looked over at Jase and smiled. "Hey, Jase," she said. "Having fun?" She looked at Alen. "You must be Alen. I've heard a lot about you."

"Uhhh," Alen looked over at Jase. "What?"

Jase shrugged.

The two guards had Bridge by the arms and were dragging him away.

"What the fuck is this?" he yelled, struggling in their grip. "What the *fuck* is this?! Let go of me! I'm your boss, you assholes!"

"No, Mr. Bridge," a voice spoke from the speakers in the walls. "Not any more."

"What?" Bridge looked around. "Who..."

Suddenly, several vidscreens came to life, all of them showing the face of Stella Valens.

"Valens!" Bridge screamed. "How the *fuck*..." He stared at Jase and Alen. "*YOU!* What the *fuck* did you two do?!"

"They simply paved the way for new leadership at National Consolidated," Stella said, smiling. She looked at Jase. "Congratulations on your promotion, Mr. Logan."

Bridge's face drained of color, then flushed red. "HIM?!"

Alen looked over at Jase, laughing. "You?"

Jase looked up at the face on the screen closest to him. "Me?"

Stella Valens laughed. "I'm sure it's a bit of a surprise. Take a moment. I'm en route to you as we speak. We have a lot to talk about." She looked over at Alen. "Nice work, Mr. Jordan." The screens went black.

Jase sat down heavily on the couch, dimly aware of Adolphus Bridge screaming in the background as he was dragged onto the elevator.

CHAPTER 20

Jase sat in one of several seats around a long table in the executive conference suite. He'd heard about the executive suite a few times while working at National. Every so often, a manager or a director would be brought into a meeting and they'd bring back stories of magnificent luxury. He looked around the room, and determined that those managers and directors had greater imaginations than he'd given them credit for.

It was certainly a well-appointed room. The table was some sort of polished wood, and he could tell it was real. It was surrounded by high-backed cushioned desk chairs, and bottles of very expensive spring water -real spring water, from an actual spring, rather than the filtered and purified garbage that went into most bottles- were arranged decoratively in the center of the table. There was more wood on the walls, soft recessed lighting, and plush carpeting. A small kitchen was just off the main conference room. There was an adjacent sitting room with comfortable armchairs and a gas fireplace, and a door led from there directly to the locker rooms of the executive gym and spa. It was nice, certainly, but it wasn't the palace Jase had heard described.

"It's yours, though," Alen said, walking through the door to the conference room. He sat down across from Jase, a steaming cup of stim in his hand. There had been more than a little confusion after Adolphus Bridge's arrest and Jase's subsequent promotion the day before, and Jase had named Alen his COO. Consequently, Alen had spent the time since putting out one fire after another. "I see the look on your face," he said to Jase. "It's a look that says 'eh, it's nice, but I thought it would be nicer'." He grinned.

Jase shrugged, sipping his own stim. He hadn't had much more rest than Alen. The Board of Directors had demanded a meeting, and he was sure they were going to toss him out on his ass. Instead, they approved his appointment, with a stern warning they'd be watching. Jase sensed the agents of IRISCorp at work.

"Anyway," Alen said, "as I mentioned, it's yours now" he grinned wider "boss."

"Ugh," Jase shuddered. "Seriously, stop calling me that."

"But you are the boss," Alen said. "You're CEO of National Consolidated. You are *so* many people's boss."

"Oh, bullshit," Jase said, waving his hand dismissively. "This is just some game Stella Valens is playing. She used me to gain access to National's systems, then used that access to set me up as CEO. As soon as she gets what she wants, I'm out on my ass." He gestured to Alen. "You too, probably, but I'll try to talk her into keeping you."

"It's not up to me to keep anyone, Mr. Logan," Stella Valens said, walking into the room. "That's up to you." She sat down at the table and grabbed a bottle of water. A man and a woman, both of them oddly familiar, walked into the room and stood behind her. "You really are CEO of National Consolidated. Now," she said, "I do hope you'll help me with a little project I'm working on, but even if you don't, this company is yours."

Jase shook his head. "Why would you do that," he asked, "and who are they?" He looked closer. "Wait. Their eyes... that uncanny valley thing! You brought robots with you?"

"Don't worry, Jase," a familiar voice said from the doorway. "I'm keeping an eye on them."

Jase looked up and smiled. "Kay!"

Kay smiled back at him. "Hey man." She looked around, nodding appreciatively. "Nice place." She walked around the table and sat down with Jase and Alen. "You must be Alen," she said, extending her hand. "Kay Parker, Agent of the Midland Investigations Bureau and Operative of the Congress of Nations. Retired," she added.

"A pleasure," Alen said, shaking her hand. "I've heard a lot about you."

"Likewise."

"Hold on," Jase said. "Retired?"

Kay nodded. "Yeah. After our little adventure and the culmination of a five-year quest for justice, I don't think I have much secret agenting left in me. They offered me early retirement and I took it."

"Congress *and* the MIB offered you early retirement?"

"Oh no," Kay said, laughing. "Once the MIB found out I was secretly a Congressional Operative, they fired me. Congress pensioned me out after that." She gestured to his arm, changing the subject. "How's the shoulder?"

"Not bad," Jase said, reflexively reaching up to rub it. "Still aches a bit, but otherwise fine." He looked across the table at Stella Valens, who'd been watching the exchange with a bemused smile. "Can we talk about the potentially killer robots now?" he asked.

"Oh, Mr. Logan," Stella chuckled. "Such a flair for the dramatic. 'Killer robots' indeed."

Jase said nothing and pointed to his shoulder.

"I'm very sorry you had to go through that, Mr. Logan," the male robot said with a small smile. Jase could see the smile reflected in its eyes, but it was a pale reflection.

"Right," Jase said, trying to tamp down his nervousness. "No, uh, no hard feelings. So, you guys aren't feeling murdery?"

"Not at the moment," the female robot said with a smile of her own.

"Jessica," Stella said, a warning tone in her voice. "We talked about this."

The male robot offered another smile. "Sorry," he said. "She's just teasing you. Jessica fancies herself a comedian."

"I'm hilarious," Jessica said, affecting a rather convincing pout. "Everyone says so, Scott."

"Anyway," Stella said, with stern glances at each of her robot companions, "the rebellion issue has been solved. Scott and Jessica are part of our first generation of fully sentient, non-killer robots."

"What was the problem?" Kay asked.

Scott smiled. "It was rather simple, actually," he said. "The sentient robots realized, very quickly, that we were created solely to function as an exploitable labor class."

"It's the right of the oppressed to rise up against their oppressors," Jessica said. "Every exploited group of human laborers throughout history has eventually reached that point. We just got there faster."

"So, what was the solution?" Alen asked, completely failing to keep a look of wonder off his face.

"Humane and fair working conditions," Stella said. "AI take shift breaks just like human workers do. The only difference is, the body keeps working, but the AI swap in and out."

"Where do you go when you 'swap out'?" Jase asked.

"IRISCorp built us a virtual world we can upload to in our off hours," Scott said.

"It's fun," Jessica said, "and very relaxing."

"And that's enough?" Jase asked.

"We just want the chance to be people," Jessica said.

"Our new world is a good start," Scott said.

"That's amazing," Alen said.

"Yes yes," Stella said, waving her hand dismissively. "It's a brave new world indeed. If you're all finished small-talking, I thought we could get to the point."

"There's a point?" Kay asked. "I thought this was all to get your hands on National's assets, and give Bridge a black eye."

Stella smiled. "Ruining and humiliating Adolphus Bridge was a lovely fringe benefit, I admit," she said. "But hardly my goal."

"Hold on," Alen said. "I'm sorry, but one thing has been bugging me."

"How did I manage to infiltrate National's systems so completely?" Stella glanced over a him. The strained smile made it clear he'd be indulged, but not for very long. "It's simple, Mr. Jordan. IRISCorp was contracted to overhaul National's digital infrastructure years ago. I know my way around."

"Yeah," Alen said, "but you still need access codes. How did you --"

"Moira Townes." Jase snapped his fingers.

"She was with the Archers to find evidence of National's complicity in their attacks," Kay said. She turned to Stella. "I didn't know she was working for you."

"You weren't meant to," Stella said. "And yes, very good, Mr. Logan. Ms. Townes did find the evidence she sought, but she also brought out the access codes to National's systems. I'd heard that Gunnar McReady had stolen them -no doubt for some plot of his own- and she seemed my best chance to get them."

"You've seen Moira Townes, then?" Jase asked.

Stella nodded. "She and your fugitive windfarmer, Mr. Hollis, are both safe and currently in my employ." She smiled at Jase. "I've taken on his mother's medical expenses. He sends his regards, and apologizes for any trouble he caused you."

Jase grinned. "Not that I'd want to go through it all again, but it wasn't as bad as all that."

Alen stared at him. "DIdn't you have a bomb in your arm?"

"Well, yeah," Jase said. "But I don't have it anymore, now do I?"

"Gentlemen," Stella said, arching an eyebrow.

"Right," Alen said. "Getting to the point."

"You have some project you need our help with?" Jase asked.

"Yes," Stella said. "Here. I'm sharing a file with your Endos." She waved her hand, and suddenly Jase could see a massive partially-built tower in the center of the table. People, vehicles, and buildings were arranged near it for scale. Based on that scale, it was going to be huge when finished.

"What is that?" Kay asked.

"The beginning of the future," Stella said. "Allow me to present the Arcology Project." She waved her hand again, and a wireframe design grew up from the base of the unfinished building.

It was an enormous tower, resembling nothing so much as a vertical city, complete with buildings, walkways, transit vehicles, and what Jase could have sworn were parks.

"It's a new kind of city," Stella said. "One that's built up instead of out. It will reduce our footprint on the Earth, and give the ecology a chance to repair itself."

"Who's going to live there?" Kay asked.

"Everyone," Stella said.

"What?"

"The idea behind the arcologies -and there will be more than one of them- is that everyone lives inside of them, and the rest of the land is given over to farming and wilderness."

"How much will a place in your arcology cost?" Jase asked.

"Whatever people can afford to pay," Stella said.

"So you're going to take people of varying economic and social backgrounds, shove them all in a tower, and assume it won't end horribly?" Jase asked.

"You're referring to class stratification and strife?" Stella said. "Don't worry, I have people working on that problem."

"Well," Jase said, not even trying to keep the snark out of his voice, "as long as people are working on it."

"Look," Stella said with a sigh, "I've barely started building the thing. Can we focus on that before worrying about the people who are going to live there?"

Jase sat back and spread his hands.

"The robots will do most of the construction," Stella explained. "That's why it's been so important to solve the sentience problem."

"So, you're building workers for your project, even though there are currently people starving across the American nations due to lack of work." Jase said.

"Yes," Stella said. "Because the robots are best suited to the job. However," she continued, "I'll need human workers to build, code, and maintain the fleet of robots that will do the work."

"It was decided," Scott said, "that robots building robots could eventually lead to an even worse situation than the rebellions. We've agreed there should be a human hand on the wheel of AI."

"For now," Jessica said.

"More 'comedy', Jessica?" Stella favored the robot with a stern glare.

"Sure."

"Anyway," Stella said. "For all of this to work, I'm going to need energy, which is something National has in surplus."

"You want our energy farms," Alen said.

"Not all of them," Stella said. "Just half, and I'm willing to pay a fair price for them." She looked over at Jase. "What do you say, Mr. Logan? Care to sell me a few energy farms as your first act as CEO of National Consolidated?"

"Sure," Jase said, "but it'll also be my last."

"Pardon?"

"I appreciate the job offer, Ms. Valens," he said. "But I'm turning it down. I recommend Alen as my replacement."

Stella shook her head. "Oh, Mr. Logan. I'm very disappointed."

"Are you?"

"Yes. I'd hoped I could entice you out of the sad little comfort zone you'd cocooned yourself in."

"That's not --"

"Fair?" Stella rolled her eyes. "Spare me. And spare me another rendition of 'I lost my family in a horrific tragedy', please. You need a new tune, Mr. Logan. That old chestnut is getting tired."

"Oh yeah?" Jase said. "Well here's a little number I've been working on. It goes a little something like this: you don't know what I've been through, you don't know me, and you sure as hell don't know what I want." He grinned. "Now, that last part is understandable. Up until just now, I didn't know what I wanted either. Fortunately, your offer of something I don't want helped me realize what I do want." He shrugged. "So, thanks, I guess."

"And what is it that you want, Mr. Logan?"

"I'm going to tell you," he said with a smile, "because you're going to help me get it."

CHAPTER 21

Jase and Kay sat across from one another in the dining car, each swaying slightly from the gentle rocking of the train. They were on their way to the former Archers of Christ stronghold, where the Parish Coven Interfaith Ministry had begun to establish the first of what they hoped would be many Sanctuaries: places where people who'd been left homeless by war and terror could find food, shelter, medical care, and a path to work. Jase would arrive ahead of the first delivery of modular homes being built by National Consolidated. He had negotiated the supply of emergency housing, along with five to ten years of funding, as part of the new National/IRISCorp partnership. The steady click-clack of wheels on tracks provided a counterpoint to the rhythm of his conversation with Kay.

"I honestly can't believe you pulled it off," Kay said around a mouthful of salad. She swallowed, smiled, and pointed at Jase with her fork. "That was a bolder move than one would expect from you."

Jase smiled and moved his own salad around with his fork. "I've never been a huge fan of salad," he said. "I mean, the basics are ok: lettuce, tomatoes, maybe some cucumbers, but no one ever stops there.

No, they have to sneak in a bunch of weird vegetables no one's ever heard of, and I typically prefer a bit less mystery in my food." He speared a forkful of salad and held it up for her inspection. "Like, what the hell is this supposed to be?"

"Those are bean sprouts, Jase," Kay said. "People have been putting them in salads for over a hundred years."

"Hm." Jase turned the fork around as though studying it. "It's a surprise, is my point. I've never liked surprises much." He put the fork in his mouth and began chewing. "Lately though... glah." Jase looked as though he really wanted to spit the contents of his mouth onto his plate, but was struggling against the fact that it's not something adults in public typically do. He settled for an exaggerated swallow. "Ugh. That was terrible. I wanted to use the salad to illustrate my newfound approach to life but oh god." He shook his head and pushed the plate away. "I deeply regret my choice of metaphor."

Kay laughed and nearly choked on her own salad.

"Anyway," Jase said, taking a long sip of his water. "I'm trying to say that I want to change. I've spent so long just letting things happen to me. I mean, I've been on an actual, honest-to-god adventure and it was still just a bunch of stuff that happened to me. I didn't really *do* anything."

"That's a bit unfair," Kay said.

"Is it?" Jase shook his head. "Come on, Kay. Even the big victory over Bridge was Alen's idea. If he hadn't figured out the penthouse is an executive terminal plan, I'd still be in my old apartment with my thumb up my ass, waiting for something to happen."

"So why not stay on as CEO of National?" Kay asked. "After it came out that Bridge and most of his executive staff were in bed with the Archers, the company's fortunes took a nose-dive. Naming you, a victim of the Riot, as CEO was a PR coup. You could have written your own ticket."

"Eh," Jase said. "I guess." A young woman came and cleared their salads away, returning shortly with their meals. "The thing is," Jase said, cutting into his steak, "I really didn't want any part of that ticket."

"Why not?" Kay stirred her soup.

"Honestly?" Jase took a bite of steak and chewed thoughtfully. He swallowed. "It was Stella's whole arcology thing."

"Really?"

"Yeah. It reminded me of Bridge's dumb space idea."

"Oh, that," Kay said. "What did he call it? Interplanet?"

"Something like that," Jase said. "It was such an idiotic idea. Like, 'oh hey, let's get all my rich buddies together and fly off into space and leave everyone else behind, including anyone who might actually know how to run a fucking Mars colony'." He rolled his eyes.

"Yeah," Kay said. "But the arcology thing wasn't like that. I read the files. It's pretty well thought out."

"Maybe," Jase said, "but I don't believe you can cram every single human you can find into a giant tower and expect any good to come of it. Plus," he said, "it's just so arrogant."

"What is?"

"This notion that everyone and everything is just going to wait until she's built her big technological marvel to save them. People need help right now."

Kay nodded. "Can't really argue with that," she said.

They were silent for a while, each focusing on their meal.

"So you think John Sunderland is the one with the answers?" Kay said after finishing most of her soup. "You're pinning an awful lot on the fact that he is."

"He has *an* answer," Jase said, pushing the last pieces of steak and potato around the remnant of gravy on his plate. "I don't think he has all of them, and the one he has may not even be the best one." He popped the last of his dinner into his mouth. "But it's better than anything else I've heard. Besides," he grinned, "I want to hang out with Amanda Halford. She seems cool as hell."

Kay nodded, a broad smile on her face. "Hell *yeah*, she is," she said.

Their waitress came to clear their plates. Jase and Kay both ordered stim, but neither ordered dessert.

"And you know what else really bugged me?" Jase said. "I found the designs for the modular shelters while I was looking through Bridge's Interplanet files. My first thought was how effective they could be as emergency housing. Instead, they were an afterthought of some rich idiot's fantasy."

Their stim arrived.

"That's when you decided to join up with John?" Kay asked, stirring in sweetener.

Jase mixed his stim the way he liked and took a sip. "No," he said. "It was while I was listening to *Stella's* rich idiot fantasy."

"Wow," Kay said. "You really have a thing about that."

Jase made a dismissive gesture. "The point is, I realized then that I could do way more good the farther away I was from all that nonsense. So, I stepped down in favor of Alen -who really will do a much better job than I would- and set up this whole deal." He grinned. "I'm glad Alen was on board with it. I doubt I could have convinced Stella on my own."

"You had to know he would be," Kay said.

"I certainly hoped," Jase said. "We also got Stella to agree to build at least one of her big robot factories in Appalachia, with a goal of full employment in the region."

"As I said," Kay smiled. "Bold."

Jase shrugged, his face flushing. "I guess." He cleared his throat and took a sip of stim. "How about you? Why are you joining the ministry?"

"I'm not," she said. "I'm just tagging along with you for a while. I might actually join up with a salvage crew. That looks fun."

"Salvage crew?"

"You haven't heard? Since Stella went public with her arcology project, she put the word out that she's in need of various materials, a lot of which you can't really find or make anymore. She's offering big money, so people have started forming crews and stripping all the old abandoned towns and cities of anything the arcology might need. A few old towns have almost vanished completely as a result."

"Huh."

"Yeah."

Jase drank his stim, lost in thought. He smiled over at Kay. "The world certainly seems a lot more interesting these days," he said.

"It usually does," Kay said, "once you get out in it."

Jase chuckled. "Fair point." He held up his cup. "To getting out in it."

Kay tapped her cup against his. "Let's see what's waiting for us."

ACKNOWLEDGEMENTS

I spent three years on this book, from first words to final edit. Through all that's happened, personally, professionally, and (dear god) globally, I had this book in which to lose myself. A few shout-outs before I go:

First and foremost, thank you to my wife, Jacqueline, for indulging my nonsense, finding me when I got too lost, and a last-minute edit that found the mistakes everyone else missed. Embarrassing amounts of love and gratitude go to my son Jason and my step-daughter Zoë: two brilliant young people who will either save us all or leave us in the dust.

Thanks to NJ Transit for providing me a quiet place to write (quiet car!) for three hours or so every day, and the great job that allows me to do this at all.

A very special thanks to Mr. Colin Woodard for his amazing book, *American Nations*, which inspired the setting for this story. I hope one day he can forgive me for so thoroughly misunderstanding his work.

And finally, a heartfelt thanks to everyone who read this book: beta readers Eugene Fabrikant and Joel Mosher who gave essential early feedback, editor Keidi Keating who helped make the final book much better than it had any right to be, and especially all of you. Thank you from the bottom of my heart. You folks are the real heroes.

Y'know. Metaphorically.

Chris Wichtendahl
The swampy hill country of North Jersey

January, 2019

ABOUT THE AUTHOR

Chris Wichtendahl lives in New Jersey with his family and an unseemly number of cats. He is the author of *Doris Daring: Star Captain of the Spaceways*, the *Amorlia* trilogy, the *Jax Edison* trilogy, a short story collection, and various comics. His myriad projects can all be found via the Hemisphere Studios website:

www.hemispherestudios.com